TruthSinger

MORE JUNIOR FICTION BY ROUSSAN THAT YOU WILL ENJOY:

TruthSinger

Barbara Haworth-Attard

Cover art by Dan Clark

ROUSSAN
PUBLISHERS INC.
Specializing in YA and fiction for pre-teens

Roussan Publishers Inc. acknowledges with appreciation the
assistance of the Book Publishing Industry Development
Program of Canadian Heritage and the Canada Council in the
production of this book.

Copyright © 1996 by Barbara Haworth-Attard

Legal deposit 3rd quarter 1996
National Library of Canada
Quebec National Library

Canadian Cataloguing in Publication Data

**Haworth-Attard, Barbara, 1953-
TruthSinger**

**(Out of this world series)
ISBN 1-896184-16-2**

I. Title. II. Title: Truth singer. III. Series

**PS8565.A865T78 1996 jC813'.54 C96-900498-2
PR9199.3.H3136Tr 1996**

Book & cover design by Dan Clark

Published simultaneously in Canada and the
United States of America.
Printed in Canada

2 3 4 5 6 7 8 9 MRQ 9 8

DEDICATION

For my sons,
Jason Martin Attard
and
Jesse Scott Attard
with much love from Mom

Chapter 1

NATHAN RESTED HIS CHIN IN HIS CUPPED HAND AND stared out the classroom window. A lone, white flake of snow struggled from a January sky so gray it drained color from everything it touched. What this place needs, Nathan thought, is a good dump of snow to cover the whole, ugly town. Might pretty it up a bit. On second thought, just bury it—deep. Nothing could make this place look better. It was too *dam* ugly. Dam ugly!

Nathan smiled to himself. He could almost hear his mother saying, "No swearing, Nathan." Like she always did.

"I didn't say it with a *N* on the end, Mom," Nathan would tell her—like he always did. "It's not a swear word that way."

Besides, he only said D-A-M when he was M-A-D. Like now, sitting bored out of his brain in the seventh grade classroom in this ugly town.

U-G-L-Y. Nathan doodled the word on the lined page in front of him, stared at it a moment, then wrote it backwards. Y-L-G-U. He read it in his head. Nah! It sounded as bad as it looked. Try again. S-N-O-W he wrote, then printed the letters backwards—W-O-N-S. His lips moved silently. WONS. That was better. It was almost a word.

He grinned, remembering last night. His mother had asked him to bring the bottle of Tums from the medicine cabinet. "Here, Mom," Nathan had said, handing the bottle to her. "Have some S-M-U-T." That was one of his better *backwords* as he called them.

"Nathan! Nathan!" Miss Burtons' voice cut through his daydreaming. She sounded annoyed and the class, led of course by Todd, began snickering. Except for Katie who sat in the desk across from Nathan.

Unmoving and staring straight ahead, she resembled a stone statue found in a park. Face frozen for all eternity in one expression. If she ever smiled would her statue-face crack? He didn't know, because Katie never smiled.

She was an oddball. She wore dresses that were too large and sagged off her skinny shoulders, the material bunching out over her chest, then gathered by string at her waist. Hadn't she ever heard of blue jeans?

Nathan stared intently at Miss Burtons, trying to pretend he'd been listening all along. Miss Burtons raised her eyebrows and sadly shook her head. She wasn't buying it, but she wasn't going to make a case out of it either.

She wasn't really a bad sort, Miss Burtons, or

rather Miss SNOTRUB. SNOTRUB had occupied the top place on his backwords list for the past two weeks. Though S-M-U-T might bump it to the number two spot. Nathan hadn't decided yet.

"As I was saying," Miss Burtons continued. "Sorcerers and magicians have been around since the beginning of time."

Nathan's hand stretched out for the yellow pencil again. He couldn't help it. Gray matter was dying here. T-I-M-E he printed, then E-M-I-T. That was a good backword. You could even make a sentence of out it. EMIT TIME.

Bits and pieces of Miss Burtons' lesson filtered through Nathan's fog. "Can you tell me some names of magicians and wizards?" he heard her ask the class.

"Gandalf," came one reply. Then others spilled out. "Harry Houdini! David Copperfield! Merlin!"

M-E-R-L-I-N. Nathan's pencil moved across the page.

N-I-L-R-E-M. Good name for a heavy metal band. As he stared at them, the letters began to swell—harsh, black marks against the white paper, filling Nathan's eyes and blotting out the desk and classroom until only the printing remained—N-I-L-R-E-M.

Nathan could feel his heart pounding. Alarmed, he looked up from the paper. Air whooshed from his lungs. He could hear Miss

Burtons' voice, but the face with the lips moving was that of a man—thin, with sharply angled cheekbones, weathered brown skin, white hair, black eyes, looking right at...*him*!

Nathan tore his glasses from his nose and squinted at them. Nothing wrong there, just the usual thumbprint-and-dirt glaze.

He put them back on. Now, beneath the man's face, he could see the softer outline of Miss Burtons' cheeks and chin. It was so spooky! Nathan looked wildly about at the class busily waving arms and calling out answers. Stone-faced Katie sat staring straight ahead. Couldn't anyone else see?

"Nathan!" Miss Burtons' voice whipped his head back around. She leaned over his desk. Nathan stared at her hands using them as an anchor to hold his mind.

"This is the second time I've had to ask for your attention," Miss Burtons said. "Look at me when I'm speaking to you, please."

Nathan didn't want to look, didn't want to see that ghost face right beside his. He fearfully raised his head, then slumped back in his chair feeling weak and dizzy. Miss Burtons had her own face back again, though red and angry looking.

"Nathan, I want a written report from you on one of the magicians we've been discussing and I will expect it Monday morning," Miss Burtons told him.

The bell rang and the class sprang to life, rushing for the door. Nathan slowly closed his notebook and stuffed it into his backpack.

"That's too bad you have extra work, and on the weekend too." Katie stood by his desk.

Nathan shrugged. Why was she talking to him? She didn't speak to anyone. Besides he didn't need an oddball feeling sorry for him. He dropped his pencil case into the backpack. Maybe if he ignored her, she'd go away.

Suddenly, Katie's hand darted out and in behind Nathan's ear. He jerked his head forward, but the hand sailed in front of his nose, holding a pencil.

"Look what I found in your ear," Katie said. She dropped the pencil on the desk and walked out of the room.

Nathan stared after her. He knew that pencil hadn't been behind his ear, so where did she get it? He picked up his backpack and headed out the classroom door.

"Nathan!" Miss Burtons called after him.

Oh no! Nathan hunched his shoulders around his head and walked rapidly down the hall. He'd pretend he hadn't heard. He had to get away before she called him again.

He pushed open the heavy school door and let it bang shut behind him. Clusters of kids stood in the yard laughing and making plans for the weekend—plans that never included him. Nathan jogged out the school gates.

"Hey, Creep!" Todd and his two friends blocked the sidewalk. "Where you going so fast? Home to mommy and your weird uncle?"

Nathan's stomach sank to the bottom of his feet. He had done nothing to this kid. Hadn't even known Todd existed until two weeks ago. Nathan tried hard to be average, bland, part of the background. So why was Todd out to get him?

He pushed past the other boy and turned onto the dirt path that ran along the river. He wanted to swivel his head around to see if Todd followed, but willed his eyes forward. Show any fear and Todd would be all over him. It was hard not to look back when any minute you expected your face to be mashed into the ground. All he really wanted to do was run. Run back to the city, back to his real home, back to the way it was before, when there was Mom and him—and Dad.

He knew Mom had had nowhere to go after she and Dad split up, but surely she could have done better than Uncle Nevill. The guy was so old he was dead, but had forgotten to lie down.

Nathan stomped across the suspended footbridge that spanned the river, feeling it sway with each step. He chanced a quick glance back and let out a deep sigh. No Todd. Safe—this time.

He stopped and hung over the iron railing to

watch the water flow liquid black between frozen grass banks. The slow, steady stream made him pleasantly dizzy, soothing the anger from him. He listened to the river's song, sluggish with winter cold as it wended its way to a never ending, then suddenly remembered—he wasn't supposed to be *listening* any more.

He left the river and cut across a field. All around him Nathan could *hear* the soft whispering of life beneath frozen ground. *Hear* the harmony between earth and animal. At one time he had thought it was like this for everyone—this *hearing*.

Every living thing had its own distinct song, similar to a fingerprint revealing true identity. He could hear these songs. Had thought everyone could. Nathan still remembered trying to explain hearing to Dad. His father had stared at him strangely, then became angry, shouting at Nathan to keep his mouth shut so people wouldn't think his son was nuts. Was he nuts? N-U-T-S S-T-U-N. Maybe he was just STUN. It didn't matter anyway, he'd finished with listening.

Nathan began the steep climb up the hill concentrating on shutting down the hearing part of his brain. He tried distracting himself by studying the red, clapboard monstrosity that loomed over him—Uncle Nevill's house. It was without a doubt the strangest looking building he'd every seen.

Walls jutted out at all angles, and someone had had the warped idea of plopping a round turret down on top of it all. It wasn't any better inside with its endless, odd-shaped rooms.

Nathan trudged up the porch steps into the kitchen, shrugged out of his coat and threw it wide of its hook. He grabbed an apple from the refrigerator and clattered up the wooden back stairs. The day they had moved in, the first words out of Uncle Nevill's mouth were that boys did not use the front, carpeted staircase. Nathan had promptly stomped down them enjoying their plush thickness to find Uncle Nevill waiting at the bottom. He hadn't used the front stairs since.

Three breathless flights later Nathan pushed open the door to his room and looked inside. Of everything awful that had happened—Dad and Mom separating, living with Uncle Nevill, a crappy school, and no mus... Of everything awful that had happened it was almost worth it just to have this room for his own.

It was in the turret, not a straight wall to be seen, and so high up that if he sat on his bed only sky and birds were visible. Standing, he could see the town spread below him, peopled, but far removed. From the opposite window a large pond ringed with trees lay below the house. Nathan looked around with satisfaction. It was a room in which a person could be truly alone.

He flung his backpack to the floor, flopped onto the bed and began gnawing a fingernail. He remembered Miss Burtons' voice following him down the corridor. How much longer could he put her off? How much longer before she phoned Mom?

Chapter 2

LLIEN STOOD SHIVERING WITHIN THE CIRCLE OF THE Nine Stones. Cold wind shrieked about the ancient rocks, giving them shrill voice. They towered above him, dark gray against the lighter, misty gray of the early winter evening. Some folk whispered that the twisted stone shapes were maidens caught magically in a never ending dance. Staring at them now, Llien fancied he saw the curve of an arm, a leg, a lowered, weary head writhing within the stone. His fingers moved rapidly in the evil warding sign, though he concealed them beneath the folds of his cloak, ever aware that the King's Counsellor, Myrrd, would frown upon his need for reassurance.

Where was he, this Counsellor? Llien turned and looked about, searching for the familiar figure. *Meet me at the stones,* Myrrd had bade him, *in the hour between day and night,* and so Llien had come, huddled within his cloak, thinking longingly of the warm fire left behind at Creemore Stronghold.

During the dark months, it was not good to be out after nightfall. It was the time belonging to the nightwalkers who searched for unsuspecting souls to steal. Llien shivered again, but this time knew it to be more in fear than cold. His eyes scanned the area a second time, and he saw now what he had missed before in his haste. Beside one of the Nine Stones, branches were piled higher than a tall man's reach, readied for a torch.

Into the circle, dragging an unwieldy tree stump, came the Counsellor. He looked like an ordinary man just then, wrestling with wayward branches that scratched at his face. When he felt Llien watching, Myrrd straightened to stand thin and tall.

Narrow of face and long of nose, his thick thatch of white hair was cropped short and unfashionably high above his ears. His cheeks were clean-shaven—an oddity because as soon as any youth was able to do so he sprouted his lifebeard.

And the eyes. The Counsellor's peculiar, black eyes that could see deep into a man's soul. Looking thus, Llien told himself, no one could think this man ordinary. He was WyndCaller.

Chapter 3

Miss Snotrub was the school's choir director and she'd been asking Nathan to join. She knew he'd gone to a music school before where he had studied voice, violin and piano. Therefore, she reasoned, Nathan would be eager to be part of the school orchestra or choir. He wasn't.

So far he'd managed to find excuses to fend her off, but how much longer would she accept them? He couldn't very well tell her the truth—that music had caused his mom and dad to split up. That all their fights had centered around money; money needed for Nathan's music lessons, instruments and special school.

How could he tell Miss Burtons about Mom yelling Nathan had a real gift, and Dad shouting back Nathan should play sports not instruments—and couldn't she see she was turning Nathan into a first class wimp.

Worse, Dad was right, he was a wimp. He had tried—but the baseball whizzed by his swinging bat. The soccer ball shot wide of the goal. He was totally useless at sports.

Nathan closed his eyes hoping to shut out the

unhappiness inside him, and in his self-made darkness heard again the river's song. He knew exactly how he would wrap his voice around its low, mellow song. Except he couldn't. That was another complication Miss Burtons knew nothing about. One day he had this clear soprano voice and the next, all he could do was croak. *Croak?* Dam! Frogs could sing better than him.

He knew all about puberty—zits on your face, hair growing in your pits and, well, other places, getting stinky and the voice changing thing. You studied puberty in school. Your Mom gave you a book to read about your body and you watched the girls' T-shirts get interestingly tight, but you never really believe it will to happen to you. Until it does. Then, what a slap in the face!

Nathan swung his feet off the bed and sat staring at a black violin case propped on a chair next to the desk. He could still play it. So far as he knew puberty hadn't affected his fingers.

He crossed the room and brushed a thick coating of dust from the lid. He hadn't opened the case in a long time and wasn't going to open it now. He was finished with music, so there wouldn't be any bills or fights and Dad and Mom could be together again.

Suddenly his fingers snapped open the catches and his hands lifted the instrument from its case. Nathan stroked the violin's smooth, gleaming body, polished to autumn gold.

"Well, boy. Are you going to stand there holding that thing or are you going to play it!"

Nathan jumped. His uncle stood in the doorway watching him. The old man was so skinny that if he turned sideways he'd disappear. Sparse strands of gray hair sprouted every which way from a head sunk between stooped shoulders. Porcupine, Nathan thought, then he got angry. His music was his alone. His uncle had no right to be in his room, spying.

"Don't glare at me, boy. Play it," Uncle Nevill ordered. Nathan put the violin back in its case, surprised to see his hands trembling.

"Never mind then," his uncle said. "Never mind." He turned from the doorway and shuffled down the hall. "For a moment there, I thought you were going to play the river's song." His voice floated back to the bedroom.

"What!" Nathan exclaimed. He started to the door, but a loud *thump* on the bedroom window stopped him. He ran and looked out.

A large crow perched on the roof below his room. It must have flown into the glass. He studied it curiously, having never seen a crow that close up before. It was completely black, except for a single, white patch on its head. Bright, avid eyes gazed steadily back at Nathan, but he no longer saw the bird. He stood lost in thought. How did Uncle Nevill know about the river's song?

"Mom." Nathan wandered into the kitchen and watched his mother drain a pot of boiled potatoes. "Why do we have to live here? Isn't there somewhere else we can go?"

"Nathan, we've been through this a hundred times," his mother said irritably. "I have no money. I'm going to school and working part-time so we can eat. It seemed like a miracle to me when Uncle Nevill suggested we live with him. I don't understand why you hate it here so much." She dumped the potatoes into a bowl and shoved it into Nathan's hand. "Put these on the table, please."

"Yeah, I know," Nathan sighed. He scrunched his nose to stop his glasses' downward slide. "It's just...this town stinks, and school's awful and Uncle Nevill is so dam weird."

"No swearing," his mother said automatically.

"No *N* Mom. Doesn't count," Nathan replied.

He plopped down on a chair and pulled a newspaper in front of him, picked up a pen and began writing in the margins. D-A-M M-A-D.

"What's wrong with Uncle Nevill?" his mother asked.

"He's weird, Mom. Peculiar. Ever notice that everything about him is gray? His hair, his clothes, his skin. He's totally colorless...he's drab." Drab. The perfect word for Uncle Nevill.

"Half the time I don't even know he's alive he's so quiet, then boom he's right in front of me scaring me half to death. He's spooky," Nathan complained.

"Uncle Nevill is a bit eccentric," his mother admitted. "But we owe him a lot for coming through for us at a tough time."

"But why did you ask *him* for a place to stay?"

"I didn't," his mother replied. "It was his suggestion."

"Well, you must have written or called and told him what was going on." Nathan pointed out.

"No," His mother said. "Actually, I've had very little contact with Uncle Nevill in the last few years. Even when I was young he was just someone who paid short visits to our house. My father's uncle." She straightened up from the oven with a platter of meat. "I do know he is a world renowned concert violinist."

Nathan's head jerked up.

"Surprised you, didn't I." His mother laughed. "Guess that's where you inherited your talent. Anyway, he was always away on tour through Europe or the Orient, even Russia," she went on. "He saw you once. Shortly after you were born."

"But Mom, if you didn't tell him what was going on, how did he know you needed a place to stay?"

His mother sank into a chair and stared at him a moment. "I don't know." She shrugged. "One day there was a letter in the mail and I was desperate and well, here we are."

At that moment they noticed a figure standing in the kitchen doorway.

"Uncle Nevill." Nathan's mother jumped up from the chair. "I was just putting supper out."

"Janet," Uncle Nevill said. "I didn't ask you here to be my housekeeper. I'm perfectly capable of caring for myself."

That was one point in Uncle Nevill's favor, Nathan had to grudgingly admit, he treated Mom okay.

"I know," Nathan's mother said. "But it makes me feel like I'm helping to pay my way around here."

Uncle Nevill looked at her a long moment, then nodded, "I do see what you mean," he said.

Carrots and gravy were put on the table and they sat down.

"So school's awful." Nathan's mother spooned potatoes onto her plate, continuing the interrupted conversation.

Nathan said nothing.

"You'll find friends soon," she assured him. "Give it time. Things will get better."

Nathan merely grunted. He hadn't met anybody yet he'd want to hang around with, not that they were exactly lining up to be friends with him.

His mother suddenly lowered her fork and stared at her plate. "I'm sorry about your music school, honey, and the lessons." Tears thickened her voice. "Maybe by summer I'll be able to afford them again."

"It doesn't matter," Nathan said. "I've given up music." He stabbed a piece of meat and shoved it into his mouth.

"What!"

Nathan could see his mother was upset. Really upset. And a small part of him felt glad. Mom didn't seem to realize that not just she and Dad were separated. He was separated, too, and no one had consulted him, asked him if he agreed to *the separation*. They had hurt him. Now, he felt glad to have hurt her.

"Nathan, you have talent, real talent," his mother protested. "You just don't throw away a gift like that."

Gift! Some gift. It had caused him nothing but misery. *And joy*. The words came unbidden into his mind but Nathan ignored them.

"Uncle Nevill, tell him," Nathan's mother pleaded.

Nathan glared at her. She shouldn't be bringing *him* into this!

"Well, Janet," Uncle Nevill said. "It's really none of my business."

Dam right! But now it felt like Uncle Nevill was an ally or something. Nathan pushed away his supper plate and grabbed the newspaper and pen again. He began to print. N-E-V-I-L-L. L-L-I-V-E-N. If he took the *L* and *N* off Lliven— Nathan quickly stroked them out—he got LIVE. And if he took the *N* and *L* off Nevill, then his uncle was—E-V-I-L!

Nathan started to laugh, but stopped abruptly when a hand came down hard over his. The pen rapidly blocked out the letters E-V-I-L with heavy, black strokes. Nathan tried to jerk his hand out from under Uncle Nevill's but couldn't. The old man had surprising strength.

"Just don't make a hasty decision, boy," Uncle Nevill said.

Then as clear as if his uncle had spoken aloud, Nathan could hear in his mind—*don't meddle in things you know nothing about.*

Uncle Nevill gave a short bark of laughter and took away his hand, but Nathan's fingers clung to the pen. D-R-A-B it printed. Nathan grunted and tried to loosen his grip, but the pen stuck to him as if glued. It raced across the newspaper. B-A-R-D.

"That was a lovely meal, Janet." Uncle Nevill rose from the table.

Nathan's hand suddenly went limp and the pen dropped lifeless to the table top. He stared at the black printing on the newspaper. D-R-A-B B-A-R-D, BARD!

Chapter 4

NATHAN AMBLED ALONG THE PATH THAT CIRCLED THE pond, swinging a stick at tall, brown weed stalks. Their brittle crackling as he chopped them down was the only sound reaching his ears. He didn't mind, because it was a friendly kind of quiet, one you could fill up with thoughts, or just drift along upon.

He was heading for his favorite place, a tree with a low, wide limb that hung out over the pond, where he liked to sit and stare into the water. Had come to think of it as his own private tree.

He crossed over the small dam that backed the water up into the pond and stopped short. Todd and his two henchmen were opposite him, stomping on the thin white ice that had hardened at the water's edge. So far they hadn't seen Nathan.

He began to back away, when Todd looked up and pointed at him. *Great!* Nathan turned and sprinted back over the dam. He knew he should be brave. Should stand his ground and face Todd down, but he really hated pain, so he kept running.

As he rounded a sharp bend in the path, one foot slipped on a soggy mixture of dead leaves and wet dirt. He flew head first, sliding on his stomach in the slippery mess. A moment later a knee jabbed into his back and a hand slammed his face down into the mud. Nathan's arms flailed wildly as he fought to free himself. Cold ooze filled his nostrils and mouth. He couldn't breathe!

"Todd MacDonald! You let him go!"

Katie! Just what he needed—a witness to his humiliation. At least she had distracted Todd so the boy's grip relaxed. Nathan raised his head and gulped air.

"I'll put a spell on you, Todd MacDonald, if you don't let him go. After the sun sets but before the moon rises," Katie's voice took on a sing-song chant. "your body will burn with fever. Your skin will stretch and crack, and leak yellow pus...."

Todd stood, taking his knee from Nathan's back. Nathan struggled up and wiped mud from his eyes. He saw Katie standing at the far side of the pond on the bough of—*his tree*, her long, purple coat bright against the winter colors of brown and gray. As Todd stared at her, Nathan saw a wariness steal into the boy's eyes. Surely Todd didn't believe Katie could really put a spell on him? Though she did look kind of impressive right now with arms held high above her head and coat swirling about her like a cape.

A sudden gust of wind rippled the water from Katie's side of the pond to where the boys stood, blew cold over them, then stilled. It was eerily silent, as if the whole world held its breath, waiting.

A thin, blue mist rose from the water and coiled about Katie's legs and body, smearing the clear outline of her purple coat. Nathan gulped and his heart began to thump noisily. It was just like what had happened with Miss Burtons' face in school.

He blinked rapidly, put a hand up to his eyes and discovered that his glasses were missing. Relief washed over him. No wonder everything was blurry. He couldn't see two feet without his glasses. He crawled through the mud searching for them, all the while stealing quick glances at Todd. The boy seemed hypnotized, unable to look away from Katie.

"You'll be covered in huge zits," she suddenly screeched. "And Shannon Clark will never look at you again!"

Zits! Nathan groaned in disgust. Dam! She'd ruined it! She'd been doing so great and then she'd ruined it.

He saw a glint to the side of the path and pounced on his glasses. One metal arm was bent, but he quickly straightened it, shoved them on his nose and looked across the pond.

He could see Katie clearly now. A skinny girl in a too big coat jumping up and down, shrieking and waving her arms madly. His brain must have short circuited to have thought her impressive.

Sudden movement in the branches above Katie caught Nathan's eye. Black wings spread wide, then beat the air as a large crow launched itself into the sky, swept low over the pond and the boys, then flew away. Wind sighed through the trees at its going, breaking the strange silence. Nathan watched it's flight until it disappeared. Had there been a patch of white on the bird's head?

Todd wiped his hands on his jeans. "C'mon guys," he said to his friends. "Let's get out of here. These two are a waste of time."

The boys sauntered off, turning occasionally to toss chunks of mud at Nathan as they went. Nathan looked down at himself. Dam! He was a mess. Katie jumped from the tree and ran around the pond to where he stood.

"What are you doing here?" Nathan snarled. He didn't know who he was maddest at—her, Todd or himself.

"What do you mean, what are you doing here?" Katie mimicked Nathan's growl. "In case you hadn't noticed, I just saved your life."

"I didn't ask for or need your help." Nathan spoke through clenched teeth. He headed up the path toward Uncle Nevill's house.

Katie hitched the purple coat higher on to her shoulders and followed. Annoyed, Nathan walked faster hoping to leave her behind but she stuck close to his heels.

"So your Mom works at the Foodmart," Katie said.

"Only part-time," Nathan told her. "She's going to university so she can get a better job." He didn't know why, but he didn't want this girl to think Mom's career choice was a grocery clerk.

"Oh," Katie said. "My mother works there all the time."

Nathan suddenly felt like he should apologize to Katie, but wasn't exactly sure why.

"Do you know what Miss Burtons' name is backwards?" he asked.

"What do you mean—backwards?"

"Turn her name around. Start with the *S* and end with the *B*," he explained.

Katie was silent a moment. "I get it," she said triumphantly. "SNOTRUB!"

"Now, try TUMS."

Katie snorted immediately this time.

"Some words are proper words each way, like TON is NOT and SAW is WAS," Nathan went on.

"And some," Katie said, "are the same frontwards or backwards, like BOB, TOT, DID. Palindromes."

Nathan's expansive mood deflated. He was supposed to be doing the telling and she had one-upped him again. He let go of a pine branch he'd pulled aside, happily aware of its sharp needles, but Katie calmly ducked out of its reach.

Nathan trotted up the path. This girl was like an itch in the middle of your back you can't scratch and get rid of. How did she know about palindromes? Even Mom hadn't known until he had told her.

MOM was a palindrome. There was something comforting and secure about MOM being the same frontwards or backwards. No surprises. On the other hand, DAD was the same frontwards and backwards, too, and there was nothing secure there.

"...you sing beautifully."

"What did you say?" Nathan asked. He'd only caught Katie's last words but a feeling of horror crept over him.

"I said your mother told my mother you sing beautifully. She said you were very talented and even used to go to a special music school."

Nathan stopped abruptly. Mom was going around telling people he could sing beautifully! He'd worked so hard to keep it a secret and she was going around saying things like *sings beautifully!*

He turned to the girl behind him. "Look, Katie. Don't tell anybody about my singing, okay?"

"Why?" she asked.

"No reason. Just don't!" he shouted. "Besides," he went on, "I don't sing any more. I've given up music."

"Given up music," Katie echoed. "How can you give up something that means so much to you?"

"I never said it meant so much to me."

"Well, if you were going to a special school and all, it must be a tiny bit important to you," Katie pointed out.

"Well, it isn't," Nathan replied. He scrambled up the steep hill to the house, breathing hard. Why didn't she go home?

"I see," Katie said softly.

See? What did she see? That the kids in this town wouldn't understand about music just like Dad didn't. Every one of them lived in the ice rink all winter and come summer he bet they all traded in their hockey sticks for baseball bats. If he played guitar or drums, that would be okay. But if they found out he could *sing beautifully* he'd be mincemeat. A target for every gung-ho kid out there, not just Todd. He shuddered to think what Todd would do if he knew.

It was different at his music school. He was one of *them*. Them who played instruments, sang, understood how much a person could love and need music. None of them were here. Not in this town.

"I won't say anything," Katie promised. "Todd won't find out."

"I don't care what Todd finds out," Nathan said angrily. "He doesn't scare me." But he did— big time.

"Of course he doesn't scare you," Katie agreed. "After all, he's just a tiny DDOT."

Nathan winced. Why had he ever told her about backwords? The house rose huge and awkward in front of him.

"I got to clean up." Nathan started up the porch steps.

"Wait!" Katie called.

Groaning, Nathan turned back. Two thin arms emerged from the purple coat, hands extended palms outward.

"See, there's nothing in my hands." Katie flipped them over to show the backs, then the palms again.

In a sudden blurring motion, one hand twisted and a red flower appeared between Katie's thumb and finger.

"Here you go." She held it out to Nathan. Her mouth stretched into a wide smile.

Nathan took the flower, but remained staring at Katie's face—the stone face. The smile lit her from inside, making her glow, the lank, greasy hair and sallow skin forgotten. Then, abruptly, the smile vanished and plain, ordinary Katie stood before him. She turned and ran down the hill, arms spread wide, coat billowing behind her, looking like a huge, purple bird taking flight.

Nathan studied the flower, rubbing his thumb over a velvet petal. It was real. But where on earth had Katie found a live, red rose in the middle of January? He looked at it closer. A red rose with a tinge of blue.

Chapter 5

NATHAN FLICKED IMPATIENTLY THROUGH THE television channels, then stabbed the *Off* button. He wandered around the room, picking up the newspaper, then throwing it down again. Saturday and he was bored out of his brain. Mom had to work all day at the store, and he had no friends to hang around with. He was on his own—as usual.

Crossing to the window, Nathan watched low-hanging clouds thickly swollen with the threat of snow scuttle across the sky. He considered going out, then decided he didn't feel like it. Didn't feel like chancing a run-in with Todd. Turning away from the window Nathan found himself facing THE DOOR.

THE DOOR led into Uncle Nevill's study and was always closed. At first that hadn't bothered Nathan. But as days passed curiosity whittled away at him until now all his thoughts centered on THE DOOR. Why was it always closed? What horrible secret did it conceal D-O-O-R R-O-O-D. ROOD. A shut door was definitely ROOD.

He knocked, then pressed his ear against the wood. Not a sound. In fact, now that he thought about it he hadn't seen Uncle Nevill all day. The old man must be out.

Nathan cautiously wrapped his fingers around the brass knob, but found himself strangely reluctant to twist it. He was being stupid. What could possibly happen if he opened the door? An alarm would go off? He'd get an electric shock? After all, nobody had actually said he wasn't to go in. Still—Nathan gnawed a fingernail—if the door opened, he'd take a quick peek inside, if it didn't, he'd go away and forget about Uncle Nevill's study forever.

He turned the knob and the door swung open. Heart thumping, Nathan poked his head in, looked quickly around, then slid the rest of his body into the room.

A large desk stood in the middle of the study. Nathan trailed his fingers over its top, enjoying the wood's warmth, then glanced up and saw the far wall. Floor to ceiling shelves were filled with musical instruments. Nathan started across the room when a sudden, painful jolt shot up his leg. Alarmed, Nathan looked down and saw his foot rested on top of a gray, rectangular shape set into the brown, wood floor. Maybe Uncle Nevill *had* wired the room with an electric alarm!

He raised his foot and the pain immediately stopped. Crouching, Nathan studied the inset. It was stone; its surface pitted and scored, ancient looking. He brushed his fingers over it and the tips went numb. He quickly snatched them away and shook his hand until feeling returned.

He could see now there were nine stone fragments, all different shapes and sizes, set in the floor in a large circle. Nathan carefully edged his way around the outside of the ring. He wasn't chancing getting fried.

Arriving safely at the shelves, Nathan forgot the stone fragments as he gaped at the instruments in front of him. He counted three small harps on the upper shelf and a larger one standing on the floor. An assortment of wind and string instruments sat on the middle shelf, all so old and odd-looking Nathan decided they must be antiques.

The lowest shelf held drums of varying styles and sizes and, tucked beneath them, a row of instrument cases, small and large. Nathan stared at the sheer number of instruments. They must be worth a fortune, and Uncle Nevill did not even keep the room locked! Anyone could walk in. *Like he had?*

Carefully skirting the stone circle again, Nathan squeezed his way behind the desk. He plopped down in the leather armchair drawn up to it, swivelled around a couple of times, then noticed a paper spread across the desktop. It appeared to be a map, but he couldn't make much sense of it. There were none of the familiar red or brown markings that indicated roadways, though his finger followed a winding blue line to its end in a large pool of the same blue. A river, he guessed, emptying into a lake or ocean. Uncle Nevill must be planning a trip.

Next to the map were several sheets of paper. Nathan shuffled through them. Some had the various phases of the moon drawn on them, others, black ink sketchings arranged in circular designs. More circles! They looked a bit like horoscope symbols. Maybe Uncle Nevill was an astrologer, could predict whether or not Nathan would survive the next year with Todd and Dad and all. Then again, maybe he'd rather not know.

He swung the chair sideways and saw the bottom drawer of the desk ajar. A black folder lay inside. Nathan stared at it a moment, then lifted the folder and set it on the desk in front of him. With the tip of one finger he eased the flap up and peered inside, then, eyes wide, quickly flipped the folder fully open.

A music manuscript, brittle and yellow with age, lay before him, though he'd never seen music written like this. Notes were scattered haphazardly over the page, thin and spidery-looking. There was no time signature, no clef sign and no staff. Between the notes was writing—of a sort—a string of recognizable letters broken here and there by drawings similar to those on the horoscope papers. Nathan tried to sound the letters out, but could not tell where one word ended and another began. They were worse than his backwords.

He turned his attention back to the notes. He could hear them clamoring in his mind, demanding to be put into order. He lowered his head over the manuscript, concentrating. A pattern began to emerge. He could almost hear it...but no...the melody remained elusive. Baffled, Nathan leaned back in the armchair.

"It is a difficult piece."

Nathan jumped, banging his shin on the open drawer. In the shadows at the far end of the room, Uncle Nevill sat in a chair calmly sipping a drink. With a final swallow, he placed his cup on a table and heaved himself up.

"Shall we take a stroll," he suggested. He crossed to the wall of instruments. Nathan held his breath as he watched the man walk directly through the stone circle—but nothing happened, not even a tiny explosion. Uncle Nevill selected an instrument case, tucked it beneath his arm and beckoned to Nathan to follow him from the room.

Nursing his bruised leg, Nathan limped behind, grabbing his jacket as they passed through the kitchen. Uncle Nevill stopped in the porch to button his overcoat and perch a cap on his head, adjusting two flaps over his ears before fastening a strap beneath his chin. Add a pair of goggles, Nathan thought disgustedly, and the old man would look like a World War I pilot. Uncle Nevill totally confused him. The old guy had been there the whole time watching him snoop around, but he hadn't said anything. Was he angry?

Uncle Nevill sniffed the cold air appreciatively, settled the instrument case securely beneath his elbow, and started briskly down the hill toward the pond. Well, he didn't act mad, but then Nathan didn't know what mad type Uncle Nevill was. The bang-the-pots and slam-the-doors type like Mom, or the yelling and poking-a-finger-in-your-face type like Dad. Or, Nathan thought uneasily, Uncle Nevill could be the worse type—the kind that used carefully selected words that sliced you into ribbons.

"Biscuit?" Uncle Nevill shoved an Oreo into Nathan's hand without breaking stride, then reached into his pocket and brought out a second. "A weakness of mine, I'm afraid," he said happily. He pried the cookie apart and popped one half into his mouth.

Watching him, Nathan began to relax. No way could a person be angry while eating the middle of an Oreo.

"Could you hear the song?" Uncle Nevill asked suddenly.

Nathan started at the unexpected question, but

knew exactly what his uncle meant.

"No," he replied. feeling frustrated all over again. He'd been reading music for years. It should have been easy.

Uncle Nevill nodded but said nothing further. He stopped by a tree growing tall beside the pond, placed his hand gently on its trunk and closed his eyes. A gone-away look appeared on his uncle's face and Nathan suddenly knew that this was how he looked, when he was *listening*. Like Uncle Nevill.

"Oak." His uncle's eyes flew open and he gave the tree an affectionate pat. "Always stand next to an oak. Refreshing. One of the reasons I settled here; the profusion of oak trees."

He continued walking quickly along the path edging the pond, popping cookies into his mouth, black eyes darting ceaselessly, missing nothing. Nathan hurried to keep up. Wasn't this guy supposed to be old? He threw sidelong glances at his uncle. So he was a world famous musician. He sure didn't look the part. A world famous musician should be tall, with long, silver hair and a commanding presence. Not this wizened, gray old man demolishing Oreos.

Nathan crammed a cookie into his mouth. Should he listen, try to find his uncle's song? He didn't like tapping into another person's song. It left him feeling depressed and out-of-sorts for days afterwards. Still — he glanced at the old man

— Uncle Nevill was too much of a mystery to pass up. Nathan swallowed the last of the chocolate biscuit, forced his body to relax and directed his listening toward his uncle. Instantly, he found the man's song.

Discordant and harsh, it tore into Nathan's hearing. He winced and fought frantically to shut it out, but he couldn't leave the song. Forced to listen, he slowly began to hear the true melody hidden beneath the first excruciating notes. The song soared within him, ancient and ageless, born from a time before time. Just as Nathan feared his mind would explode in ecstacy, the song abruptly ended, like a wall suddenly erected closing him out of his uncle's mind. Nathan ran a shaking hand across his forehead and felt it slick with cold sweat. His legs trembled.

"You should be careful doing that," Uncle Nevill said sternly. "You have no training or shielding. I allowed you in and took you out before any damage was done. You listen to someone who is not so kindly disposed and you could be left without a mind."

Nathan stared at him. No one had ever known when he'd tapped into their song before; until now. What did Uncle Nevill mean—training and shielding?

"You have been given a wonderful gift," Uncle Nevill continued.

Nathan wondered if he was talking about music or—or the other.

"If you do not use it, you will eventually lose the ability to do so."

Again Nathan was uncertain what Uncle Nevill was referring to. But it didn't really matter. He didn't know why he had listened to his uncle's song. A moment of weakness he supposed. He had promised himself there would be no more hearing, no more music. He had already written his father that he'd stopped his lessons and pretty soon Dad would call and everything would be fine again, like before.*Except you will have no music.* The sad words echoed in Nathan's mind, probing the dark, hurting place in his heart.

Uncle Nevill stopped abruptly and slapped his hand against another tree trunk. Jumping at the unexpected crack, Nathan saw a familiar, low limb stretched out over the pond. *His* tree!

"My favorite spot," Uncle Nevill said, gazing up into the maze of branches.

Nathan groaned. It seemed *his* tree was everyone's favorite spot. Uncle Nevill rested the instrument case in a *V* where two branches met, and removed a violin and bow. He tuned and tightened, then nodded his head in satisfaction as he settled the instrument securely beneath his chin and began to play.

Sweet and clear the violin sang, its voice

floating over the water in a haunting song. Nathan's eyes widened. He recognized it. It was the song from the manuscript.

As the last pure note faded to silence, sadness and longing welled up in Nathan. An overwhelming feeling of loss swept over him; for Dad, for Mom, for music and mostly, for himself. He stared at his uncle who stood face raised to the sky as if in silent converse, violin and bow still. Where had such a song come from? Not from here.

Chapter 6

"NATHAN! IT'S DAD FOR YOU."

"Great." Nathan grabbed the phone from his mother. "Hi, Dad. What time are you coming on Friday?"

Finally, Dad and Nathan were to spend next weekend together. And that was just the beginning. Dad would see that Nathan had changed; had grown a couple of inches, put on a few pounds. And when he came to pick Nathan up, Dad and Mom would meet and realize how much they missed each other and that would be that. They'd all be together again.

"...something came up."

"What's that, Dad?" Nathan had been so busy planning the reunion, he'd missed most the conversation.

"I said something came up and I can't make it this weekend," his father repeated. "Besides, the apartment's so small we'd be falling over each other. I'm planning to move to a bigger one soon and I think we should wait until then to get together."

Nathan slammed the phone down. Something came up? Like what? What could be more important than seeing his son? Anything, obviously. Nathan's dream family splintered into fragments too small to be mended. Dad didn't want to see him.

"Damn!" The word erupted from deep inside Nathan.

"Nathan. It's not you. It's him," his mother said.

Nathan blinked, unable to see her clearly through a growing, red haze of anger.

"You're right!" he shouted. "It's not me. It's *you!* You made Dad leave. I heard you tell him to go. It's your fault. You don't even want him to come back, do you?"

"No, I don't." His mother's voice was firm. "It's not going to happen, Nathan. Don't harbor hopes that your Dad and I will be together again. I have my own life now."

Her own life! Nathan wanted to kick something. She had her own life. So where did that leave him? What was his life? Pathetic! That's what. No friends, a stupid school, a kid who wanted to pulverize him, a weird girl following him around—pathetic!

"Go ahead then. Enjoy *your* life, but don't expect me to be part of it." Nathan knew his words stabbed into his mother, but he didn't care. Why should he be the only one to bleed? That was how it felt inside, like a large, bleeding wound.

"Nathan!" Uncle Nevill's voice boomed through the kitchen. His body filled the doorway.

Nathan shrank back. How had he ever thought Uncle Nevill old and frail? He whirled, grabbed his coat and ran out the door.

His mother called after him, but Nathan kept running down the hill away from the house. The muscles in his legs protested and his lungs ached for air, but Nathan forced his body to keep going. Finally, at the edge of the pond his exhausted legs gave out and he fell heavily. He lay on his back, gasping, feeling his face wet—with sweat or tears, he didn't much care which.

He'd said such awful things to Mom. But—a hard lump swelled in his throat—why should he feel bad? She obviously didn't care about him.

A black dot wheeled high above him in the gray sky. Another crow? C-R-O-W. He pictured the letters in his mind, then turned them backwards. W-O-R-C. WORC. Sounded like a creature from a fantasy; evil with a sharp beak for ripping and tearing. A shiver crept up Nathan's spine. He was scaring himself, but it beat thinking about what had happened at home. Besides, he'd rather face a WORC than Mom right now.

He stood up, groaning at the stiffness in his legs, and looked out over the pond. A couple of cold nights had rimmed it with white ice, though Nathan could see black, open water beyond. He placed one foot on the ice and pressed down. It seemed solid enough. He jumped with both feet. A sharp crack split the air, but the ice held so Nathan inched his way forward.

"That's about the stupidest thing I've ever seen anybody do," Katie shouted from behind him.

Nathan groaned. What did that girl have— radar? Wherever he went she turned up, as welcome as a wart. But she was right, the ice wouldn't hold him.

He turned to start back when he saw Todd and his friends leaping down the hill behind Katie. Nathan felt his glasses slide down his nose, but he ignored them. He had no choice now. He couldn't chicken out in front of Todd. He had to go on.

He shoved his glasses back in place and began to shuffle over the ice toward the black water. He'd just go to the edge to show them. Yeah— right! Show them how fast he could drown! The ice sagged beneath his feet. *Damn!*

He heard then the song of the ice urging him on, promising safety. Fear and caution fled. Nathan stepped forward confidently, then too late heard the truth. It wasn't the ice that called him, but the open water. He tried to step back but his feet kept sliding forward and cold water seeped around his ankles.

Nathan looked frantically at the shore. Maybe if he ran real fast... Todd picked up a huge rock, raised it above his head and dropped it on to the ice. Chunks of white flew as the rock crashed through and sank. Nathan's heart sank with it. He'd never get back now.

He saw Katie's arms slowly rise. Tendrils of blue mist rose from the white ice, curled about her wrists and dripped from her fingers. Nathan gasped, finding it difficult to breathe, as if frigid water already filled his lungs. Colors receded until all that reached Nathan's eyes were white ice and black water.

Suddenly Nathan felt light, weightless, like his body no longer had substance. Feet dangling, he floated above the ice, drifting toward the shore. Upon gaining firm land he stumbled, his legs abruptly bearing weight again.

Todd's eyes narrowed. "How'd you do that?" he asked.

"It's all in where you place your foot," Nathan mumbled. He didn't look at Katie. She'd done that—floated him over the ice. But how?

A sudden gust of wind swirled brown leaves about their feet, growing in intensity until the trees tossed wildly. Todd continued to stare; first at Nathan, then at Katie, then slowly backed away.

"You're both nuts," he said. Signaling the boys to follow, he climbed up the bank.

Nathan looked out over the pond and stared, horrified to see the broken white ice laced with black water. There was no way he had walked over that! He should be dead—except for Katie.

He turned to speak to her, but found he was alone. He stood a moment undecided. He didn't really want to go home yet, and he did want to talk to Katie. He had never been to her house but had overheard the kids talking about the Spencer place down by the railroad tracks. It shouldn't be too hard to find.

He trudged down the path away from the pond and crossed the footbridge, fighting wind that pushed solid against him. Thrusting hands deep into his pockets for warmth, Nathan continued along the asphalt road until it became gravel. Here the wind threw tiny stones and dirt into his face. Strange, Nathan thought as he pulled his coat collar up around his stinging cheeks, a windstorm hadn't been forecast today.

He debated returning home but saw he had arrived at the tracks and, crossing them, found a rusted mailbox dangling from a post with the faded letters E-N-C-E-R painted on the side. A lane with two deep ruts led into a snarl of undergrowth. Nathan started down it, stopping at a huge yellow and black sign—*NO TRESPASSING*. He hesitated a moment, shrugged and continued on. Rounding a curve, he found himself facing a second sign—*GUARD DOGS ON DUTY.*

He peered down the road. What exactly were the dogs guarding? The tired-looking, old house that stood at the end of the lane? It appeared deserted. Missing panes of glass had been stuffed with cardboard and the porch roof had collapsed at one end. Wind whistled through the rusted skeletons of old cars and farm machinery littering the yard. It gave him the creeps. No one could possibly live here. He must be at the wrong place.

Nathan turned to leave when from the back of the house, two large dogs bounded barking fiercely. Nathan froze. His feet couldn't move. The first dog reached him and lunged. Nathan shut his eyes.

"Stop!"

Nathan heard panting nearby, felt something hard knock against his leg, but the anticipated sinking of teeth into skin didn't come. He slowly opened one eye. A dog prowled around in front of him, growling deep in its throat. A second one circled behind, curled lips baring sharp teeth.

"Whatcha doing here? Can'tcha read the sign?" A man in a dirty T-shirt stood swaying in front of him, a bottle of beer in his hand. Liquid slopped out as he gestured toward the lane.

"I...I came to see Katie," Nathan stammered.

The man lurched closer and stuck his face into Nathan's. "Well, she ain't seeing you, so git yerself out of here," he snarled.

Nathan flinched at the man's sour breath. Was he Katie's father?

"Git now, like I said. B'fore I sic them dogs on ya." More liquid foamed from the bottle as the man flung his arm toward the animals.

Nathan turned and fled down the path. He glanced back once and saw a crowd of white faces pressed against the one remaining pane of glass. His feet flew around the curve when a hand reached out and grabbed his shoulder. Nathan yelped and struggled to get away.

"Stop it!" A voice hissed. "It's me."

Nathan went limp and Katie let go of his sleeve.

"I thought it was that guy," Nathan panted.

"My dad?" She shrugged. "He couldn't walk this far the shape he's in."

So the drunk guy was her father.

"What are you staring at?" Katie demanded.

Nathan shook his head. "Nothing."

"So what are you doing here? Come to check me out like all the others?" She sounded hard and defensive.

"No..." Nathan's voice trailed off. "I wanted to know how you did it," he said finally.

"Did what?" Katie asked. The wind whipped strings of hair over her face.

"I should have drowned. That ice couldn't hold me," Nathan said flatly. "But you got me out of there."

"Don't be silly." They were both shouting now over the wind's howl.

Katie's face retreated to its stone stillness, then unexpectedly crumpled. Tears slid down her cheeks. She pushed Nathan into the shelter of a fallen tree trunk. He looked up nervously at the tangle of branches creaking and swaying high above him.

"I don't know how it happens," Katie whispered. Her eyes were huge. "I saw you were going to fall through the ice. Then I thought to myself that the only way you'd get back was if you had wings. Next thing—you were floating over the ice toward me. It's happened before, you know. I think something and it comes true." She gulped. "The worse thing is, when Todd was breaking up the ice, I wished *he* was out there instead of you and I knew I could put him there, but somehow I managed to stop the thought before anything bad happened."

She sniffed and wiped the back of her hand across her nose. "But..." She took a deep breath. "What if next time I can't stop the thought, and I hurt someone?"

Nathan stared at her. Was she a poltergeist or something Then again, what was he? He could *hear* songs.

"Did you see the way they looked at me?" Katie went on. "Todd and those guys? They're scared of me. *I'm* scared of me."

"It's because you're different," Nathan said.

Katie's head swung up and she glared at him. "So, what's wrong with different," she demanded.

"Nothing. Nothing," Nathan stammered. Dam! She was so changeable. And he didn't want to make her mad. Who knew what she'd do to him.

"I've been different all my life," Katie told him. "Anyone can be the same, being different is special." She peered closely at him from beneath dirty, knotted hair."You're scared of me."

Nathan began to shake his head, then stopped. "A bit," he admitted. "But I do know what you mean. I'm different too. I'll explain it to you some day when you have lots of time."

They sat silently for a while.

"You saw him that day, didn't you?" Nathan asked suddenly.

"Saw who?"

"At school the other day. Miss Burtons' face changed and someone else's face, a man's, took over. You saw it, too," Nathan repeated.

Katie looked ready to deny it, then her shoulders slumped. "Yeah. But what did you want me to say. *Did you see that face*? In the middle of class? People already think I'm half-crazy.

"I've seen him before," she added. "Since I was little. I used to think he was my guardian angel, until I realized he stunk at that job. Now...I don't know what I think."

Nathan was quiet a moment. "There's someone I want you to meet," he said finally. "Someone I suspect is different, too."

Katie studied him a moment, then her mouth stretched in a wide grin. Nathan gaped. It was incredible how her face changed when she smiled. Made her almost—beautiful. It left him feeling like he'd been given a wonderful gift. The smile faded, and skinny, plain Katie stood before him. Must have been the shadows beneath the trees that made her look that way, Nathan decided.

A raucous squawking whipped Nathan's head up in time to see a black missile launch itself from the top of a tree and dive toward them.

"Look out!" he yelled.

He pushed Katie down and flattened himself against the ground, feeling the hair on his head stir as the crow skimmed over them, then flew off. Had Nathan glimpsed a flash of white?

"That one's a WORC."

Chapter 7

LLIEN GRUNTED AND HEAVED THE STUMP ON TOP OF the pile of wood. Up close it towered higher than he'd first thought.

"What is happening, Counsellor?" he asked.

"I am performing a summoning," Myrrd replied.

Llien looked again at the stacked branches. So that was the reason for its great size, for something as important as a summoning.

"The fire is for warmth as I expect we'll be here some time and the night will be cold," Myrrd said mildly.

Red flooded Llien's face. Always he was made to feel foolish. At least this time no one had witnessed his embarrassment.

He should leave. Nothing forced him to stay. No contract bound him to the King's Counsellor. He believed himself fifteen years grown, or near that he guessed. His voice had deepened, a thin down covered his cheeks and his chest had broadened from that of boy to man. There was no need to stay on as servant, apprentice, or whatever his position, to Myrrd any longer. He owed the man nothing and anything that might have been due had been repaid long ago.

Then Llien remembered again, as he had many times before, the Counsellor's tall figure plunging through smoke to pull him free of the burning cottage. Remembered a cloak wrapped securely about his small body and gentle arms carrying him past the man and woman lying unmoving on the doorstone. Away from certain death by fire, starvation, wild beasts, or worse, human enemies. Those same arms had soothed him when he screamed with nightmares and cooled his childhood fevers.

When he got older, Llien had served the Counsellor. Cleaned boots, mended torn clothes and harness, and prepared drink and food. He had sat teeth chattering from night cold while Myrrd taught him star patterns and moon faces. And he waited. Rain lashed him as the Counsellor explained the blue white lightning bolts that split the sky. Hot sun beat down on his back as he gathered healing plants and roots, then spent long hours grinding them to powder for the Counsellor's use. And he waited.

He could recite a long history of kings, add a column of figures, though he could not yet fully master the symbols called writing. And so twelve winters had passed and still he waited.

The King's Counsellor was feared and

respected throughout Angliocch. Advisor to the High King, there were none above him except the King, and at times Llien even questioned that. He had soon discovered that being the Counsellor's companion had certain advantages. A single word set the best food, ale, beds and clothing before him. A cold glance cowed the servants and sent them scurrying to do his bidding. The fear in their eyes delighted him. He was a man to be feared. He was successor to WyndCaller.

Unfortunately, Myrrd preferred his simple wood hut in the center of the forest to the spacious strongholds of the highborns and spent much time there. Here, Llien had to do for them what the lowest servants did. Life felt flat and sour when there was no one to order about. When he became WyndCaller, Llien vowed, he'd build the largest stronghold in the land and live there in comfort. When he became WyndCaller.... That was why he did not leave.

He watched the Counsellor pace four strides in every direction, stopping at each turning to mutter and raise an arm. A blue symbol appeared briefly on the air sketched by Myrrd's hand, then vanished. There was power here within the Nine Stones. A light breeze caressed Llien's cheek, stiffened and stirred his hair. Restlessness and discontent deepened as if carried to him on currents of air.

He had waited, endured the lessons and chores, and, he had to admit, kindness, for one thing and one thing only—to possess the ability to call the WyndMagic.

He dreamt constantly of it. Yearned for it. Could scream for the need of it and yet never in those twelve long years had Myrrd parted with even the tiniest shred of wynd knowledge.

Llien's fingers stroked the smooth skin beneath his ear. He did not even bear the mark of apprenticeship, the promise of his life-work that boys half his age carried.

He looked up from his musings and saw Myrrd watching him, a peculiar mix of sadness and compassion on his face. Llien flushed again. Could the Counsellor read a man's thoughts? At times he believed so.

"Lad," Myrrd ordered. "Light the fire, then come beside me. You'll be safe within." He gestured to where faint blue lines glimmered, outlining a rectangle in the dirt.

Lad! Llien thrust his hand deep into his carrypouch searching for the firestones. Could Myrrd not see he was a man now. His fingers fumbled, awkward from cold, and he could not pull the stones free.

"Couldn't you just make fire?" Llien demanded angrily. What was the point of being WyndCaller if you did not use the magic.

"Magic is not something to be squandered," the Counsellor told him. "Every time it is used, it has to be taken from elsewhere which leaves an imbalance and weakness. Therefore, it must be wielded sparingly. We have the proper means to light a fire, so we use it."

Despite the seeming patience in Myrrd's voice, Llien could hear the sharpness beneath and quickly pried the stones from the pouch. He clapped them together and watched sparks fall upon the wood. He cupped his hands about them, blew gently and was rewarded by a small, yellow flame. Within minutes the wood caught and Llien stepped into the rectangle beside the Counsellor.

"I begin," Myrrd announced. "Stay within the lines or I will not be able to protect you." He smiled grimly. "Not always do the proper beings attend a summoning."

He raised his arms and began to chant. The sound grated harshly on Llien's ears, but he had heard it many times before and paid the discomfort little mind. Wind whipped his cloak tight about his legs, biting and burning his fingers. He could feel the magic being called, riding to Myrrd upon the gale. Coming....He grew giddy with WyndMagic—and need. But he could do nothing. He had no knowledge of how to make the magic his own. Would it always be thus? Would he always be on the outside, never knowing how it truly felt to call the WyndMagic to him?

The sky thickened with stormclouds herded by blasts of wind and the Nine Stones disappeared beneath a shroud of blue mist. Beyond the circle of firelight Llien thought he could see ghostly dark shapes and watching eyes. Merely the flames's dancing shadows, but his mouth became dry with fear. It suddenly occurred to him that he had been so caught up in his own misery he had not thought to ask. Who exactly was WyndCaller summoning?

Chapter 8

NATHAN BURST INTO THE STUDY, TOWING KATIE BEHIND him. Uncle Nevill stood gazing out the window but turned and smiled, unsurprised by their arrival.

"Uncle Nevill," Nathan began. "This is Katie. She..." He stopped. How to explain that Katie had made him fly over the ice? It wasn't the kind of thing you just blurted out.

"I'm pleased to meet you at last, my dear." Uncle Nevill came around the front of the desk and peered at Katie with great interest.

At last? "You know her?" Nathan asked.

"I've heard a great deal about Katie," Uncle Nevill answered.

Nathan felt cheated and bewildered. Here he had been bringing Katie to meet Uncle Nevill and the man knew about her all along. Did he know everything? Maybe not this...

"She made me fly over the pond," Nathan announced. He watched his uncle's face closely, but didn't see any of the expected disbelief. "Not exactly fly," he continued. "More like drift. I mean, I wasn't flapping my arms or anything...."

He wasn't doing a very good job of telling this.

In fact, he couldn't think clearly, his brain moving sluggishly as if smothered in thick honey. Nor, Nathan blinked, could he see very well.

He glanced toward the window and saw the fading light of winter afternoon. Inside his uncle's study, though, night had already fallen; a swirling, living night. Wind tore through the room, sweeping papers before it in a mad dance. Nathan thought he could hear a voice calling, faintly as if from a great distance. Pain raced up his legs. Looking down, he was horrified to see the three of them stood within the circle of the stone fragments, stones that now pulsed with blue light.

He looked up to see the swirling night swallow his uncle's legs, then his body. Stumbling back, Nathan frantically reached for Katie. He had to get them outside of the stone circle, but his flailing hand found only empty air. Terrified, he watched as the roaring blackness bore down on him. *Damn!*

Nathan lay with his eyes clenched tight. His entire body felt flattened and sore, as if someone had sucked him through a straw, then spat him out.

Slowly he forced opened his eyelids but couldn't see a thing. One hand frantically pawed at his face to find his glasses perched on his nose. So that wasn't the problem. His teeth chattered loudly. He was freezing. Maybe he had actually fallen through the ice at the pond. Maybe he had drowned and everything that had happened since was a dream or an out-of-body experience. Maybe he was really *dead!*

Nathan scrambled to his hands and knees, wincing at a sudden painful pricking of his fingers. Puzzled, he patted the ground in front of him and felt hard, frozen stubble. He threw his head back. Stars wheeled crazily in the sky above, then a white moon slid from beneath fast moving clouds. Amazing! Death had ground, sky, stars and the moon! Who would ever have guessed...unless of course... he rolled up his sleeve and pinched the exposed skin. *Ouch!* He wasn't dead; in fact, was very much alive.

Nathan sat back on his heels enjoying a momentary elation. So if he hadn't died, what had happened? The last thing he remembered was being in Uncle Nevill's study with Katie. Then wind and darkness.

"Katie? Uncle Nevill?" he called softly, strangely reluctant to shout into the vast darkness surrounding him. No one answered.

A cloud sailed over, then away from the moon. In the fleeting splash of light, Nathan saw land stretching out before him, flat and unbroken by a barn or house or any other buildings. Also missing, he realized, was the ever present drone of traffic. No sound reached his ear except a muted roar like waves breaking on rocks. But the pond wasn't big enough for one small wave, let alone this constant pounding.

Nathan sniffed. The air smelled great. Clean and sharp, no gas or chemical fumes, only a trace of woodsmoke. Maybe he had amnesia. Had wandered outside and become lost. Good theory, except he remembered his name; remembered Katie, Uncle Nevill—knew everything but—where. He'd have to find someone, get help.

He began to climb to his feet when a low growl came from the darkness in front of him. He slowly sank to the ground again. One of Katie's dogs? A pair of yellow eyes, wicked and gleaming, swung from side to side as if their owner was shaking its head. A very large head. Suddenly they stopped moving and narrowed. Nathan wanted to run, but the yellow eyes held him motionless, then hurtled toward him.

Nathan screamed and rolled to one side. A burst of blue light suddenly split the night and he heard a surprised yelp, followed by a howl of rage and pain. He looked up to see a large, shaggy shape poised to leap on him, then nothing, only the choking stench of burnt fur.

"We wondered where you were."

Nathan looked up to see Uncle Nevill and a white-faced Katie hovering over him. Beside them stood a strange boy. Nathan climbed shakily to his feet and saw a fourth figure, a tall, thin man who loomed above them all.

"This is Myrrd," Uncle Nevill indicated, then gestured toward the boy. "And Llien."

Nathan barely acknowledged the boy's presence. He couldn't stop staring at the man. A black cape woven of night and shimmering with silver threads of starfire swirled about him. A blue ball hovered above the man's head, casting a stark white light that reminded Nathan of fireworks that flashed and banged loudly without sprinkling the sky with color. The hair rose on the back of Nathan's neck. It was him! The guy who had taken over Miss Burtons' face!

"Are you okay?" Katie asked.

"Yeah, fine," Nathan replied. *Fine*? He was anything but fine. His teeth rattled like castanets. "Some huge dog, huh?"

"Wolf," the tall man said.

"Wolf?" Nathan snorted. "There're no wolves around Edmundston."

"I would think not," the tall man agreed, then turned to Uncle Nevill. "I am pleased to see you again, old friend. I apologize for summoning you in such an abrupt fashion, but there is an urgent matter on which I must speak to you. Things are proceeding faster than we had anticipated."

The two men began to climb a gentle hill.

"Come along, children," Uncle Nevill called

over his shoulder. "Stay close."

Nathan stumbled after Katie. "What's going on?" he asked. "Where are we?"

"I don't know," she answered. She looked dazed. "One minute I was in your house and next—I was up there." She waved a hand toward the flat-topped hill.

Nathan looked up and saw the yellow glow of a fire illuminating tall, uneven structures that rose from the hilltop. "What are those? Rocks?"

"The Nine Stones."

Nathan had forgotten about the boy who trailed after them. He stopped climbing and looked back. He had thought Katie dressed strange, this kid could win the prize for weird. Leather boots were laced to the knees where wool pants bagged over them. The boy clutched a green cloak tightly about him. Blonde hair, cut ragged across his forehead, hung long to his shoulders. A pouch was slung across his chest, secured by a leather strap. Though not much taller than Nathan, the boy appeared broader and well muscled. A sheen of fine hair on his chin suggested he was a few years older than Nathan.

"What did he say?" Nathan asked Katie. He hadn't understood a single word the boy had spoken.

She shrugged.

"The Nine Stones," the boy repeated, drawing

the words out slowly for Nathan's benefit.

Nathan felt himself bristle, though had to admit he could understand the boy this time. He was speaking English, but with a very thick accent.

"The Nine Stones?" Nathan echoed, looking puzzled.

The boy stared at him incredulously. "They are a place of great power. It is said the King's Counsellor himself brought them from over the water and set them here."

Nathan listened carefully. He didn't get every word, but thought he had the meaning. The Nine Stones were a sacred place or something, and some man had supposedly carried them here.

As the boy stepped past them to continue up the hill, his cloak fell open exposing a long knife blade. Staring at it, Nathan felt a tremor run through him.

They crested the top of the hill and Nathan saw that there were indeed nine stones set in a circle, each equally spaced as if placed with great consideration. Firelight licked at their hard surfaces, giving them the uncanny appearance of wavering life. Nathan thumped the stone nearest him.

"Oh yeah, right. Like some guy carried these here by himself," he said. "This King's Counsellor must be some strong sucker."

The boy drew himself up straight. "He is WyndCaller," he said. His eyes penetrated Nathan's, then shifted across the circle to where Uncle Nevill and the tall man stood talking.

"Is that him? WyndCaller?" Nathan asked.

The boy glared at Nathan as if discovering something disgusting found on the sole of his boot, then crossed to the fire.

"Guess I'm supposed to know who this Caller guy is," Nathan said to Katie. "Nice kid. Who is he?"

"I don't know," Katie answered irritably. "Why do you keep asking me all these dumb questions? I don't know any more than you do." She turned her back on him and stared after the boy.

Nathan ran a hand over the stone's scarred surface and was suddenly reminded of the stone insets in Uncle Nevill's study. Weren't there nine of them, too?

"These are huge," he said. "Solid. He expects me to believe one man..." His voice trailed off.

Stone should be cold, but this one felt uncomfortably warm. Nathan tried to yank his hand away, but it was stuck fast. He placed his other hand next to it and it too instantly adhered to the stone. He fought to free himself, then abruptly stopped his struggles.

The stone's song flowed through him, ancient and timeless, bearing echoes of Uncle Nevill's song. With recognition came joy, then an insatiable need to hear more. He wanted to stay here, become one with the stone.

"No!" Katie's scream startled Nathan.

He could barely lift his head or open eyes heavy with sleep and dreams. Then Nathan saw his hands. Horror jolted the languor from his body. Stone! His hands had turned to stone! The gray hardness crept steadily up his arms.

Nathan shrieked and pulled, but the stone refused to let him go. Hearing their cries, Uncle Nevill and Myrrd whirled about. Katie's hand came down hard on Nathan's shoulder.

"No!" she screamed again. "You can't have him."

Blue fire streaked down Katie's arm, exploding into Nathan's hands. Myrrd crossed the circle in a couple of long legged strides and placed his hand over Katie's. Uncle Nevill sang, urging the stone to release the boy. Nathan screamed as blue fire ate the gray from his arms and hands. Then abruptly, they fell loose of the rock and dangled at his sides.

Nathan's body trembled, and he felt faint from the agonizing pain in his arms. Katie whimpered beside him. It would be a contest, Nathan thought, to see which one of them would pass out first. Uncle Nevill rubbed Nathan's hands between his own, humming all the while, and slowly the pain receded until only a dull ache remained.

"Always one for getting in trouble aren't you." Uncle Nevill shook his head. "Come near the fire. The Ancients' songs are beautiful but chilling." He shepherded Katie and Nathan toward the hot flames.

Nathan flexed his fingers, relieved that they all seemed to be working. Uncle Nevill and Myrrd resumed their conversation, though Nathan noticed the tall man continually glance toward Katie. And, he saw, someone else appeared very interested in her too.

From the other side of the fire, the strange boy stared avidly at Katie, and Nathan didn't like his look one bit. Full of desperation, hunger, and— hate! But why would he hate Katie? He didn't even know her.

Nathan sighed. He couldn't think now. He was exhausted. He stretched his hands closer to the fire, greedy for its warmth. So Katie had saved him once again. He was pathetic. Nathan sunk into gloomy despair. He just wanted to go home. Wherever that was. He needed to talk to Uncle Nevill, but the old man was still deep in discussion with Myrrd. Finally, Nathan saw him give a weary nod and make his way toward the fire.

"Well, children," Uncle Nevill said. "There are matters here that require my attention, and I cannot risk sending you back home on your own.

Also, having performed the summoning once, Myrrd is uneasy about expending any more energy tonight.

I'm sorry you're caught in this," he continued. "But then, sometimes fate steps in and makes itself known. Perhaps this is one of those times. We'll make our way to Creemore Stronghold and see about some warm food and beds."

Creemore Stronghold? There was no place near Edmundston named that. Where were they? What were they *caught in*?

Uncle Nevill started down the hill. Dismayed, Nathan watched him go. That was that, he thought angrily. He was just supposed to follow this man who'd kidnapped him and whom he barely knew. Just do what he said. Well, if Uncle Nevill thought he could order him around, he could think again.

Nathan looked about for Katie and found that only he remained by the dying fire. The others were halfway down the hill. He shivered with cold and the memory of yellow eyes, shaggy shapes and stone hands.

Dam! "Wait up!" He called.

Chapter 9

NATHAN TWIRLED THE EARTHENWARE CUP AROUND AND around in his hand. Occasionally he raised it to his mouth and sipped. The liquid inside was fruity and sweet, not really to his liking, but it was warm and wet and he was cold and thirsty.

It had been a long, frosty walk to the stronghold. They had passed wide fields with their crops of black, frozen earth and small, windowless, grass-roofed huts huddled together within the shelter of a second immense hill. In a spell of moonlight Nathan had glimpsed a huge structure looming over them, rising from the flat topped mound as if it had grown rather than been built there. After climbing a dirt road pitted with holes, they had scrambled over an earthen wall only to find their way blocked by a wooden stockade. The King's Counsellor had pounded at the gate and upon seeing them, a guard had hurriedly opened it. They stood inside Creemore Stronghold.

Nathan estimated the stout, stone building measured approximately three stories high. He would have called it a castle, except it didn't have

fancy turrets. Yet it was bigger and more elaborate than a fort. Stronghold was a good name for it, Nathan decided. Solid and impenetrable.
Now he sat in the Great Hall of Creemore Stronghold.

He shifted on the hard, backless bench trying to get comfortable. All they had done since arriving was sit and wait, and his butt was getting mighty sore. Curiosity had long passed to impatience and anger, then to weariness and apathy. He no longer cared where they were. He just wanted to fall into a soft bed.

Except these people might not have beds. Beside the giant firepits that ran the length of the room, people slept fully dressed, boots and all, as if they had keeled over in sleep.

Nathan looked around the hall. It was the size of the school gymnasium back home, except the gymnasium did not have firepits nor the huge hearths that lined the walls, so big a man could stand upright in them. A small army would be needed just to keep the place stocked with wood, though it appeared they burned hunks of grass or something else that smoked a great deal. His eyes had been stinging nonstop since they had arrived and his throat felt tight and sore. At intervals along the walls torches burned, adding tar scented, black smoke to the thick air.

Nathan shuffled his feet through the weeds

spread over the floor—or rushes as Katie called them—and turned up a large bone. He immediately stopped moving his feet. Obviously these rushes were used as one big garbage can. No telling what other disgusting stuff he might find.

The room stunk. Even over the choking smoke smell there was a foul odor of unwashed bodies, animal droppings, grease and decaying food. Mostly Nathan tried to breathe through his mouth, but upon occasion forgot. A couple of stomach retching whiffs soon reminded him.

A dog crept over and grabbed the bone his foot had unearthed, quarreled with another dog over it, then slunk away minus his supper. Dogs, people, all jumbled together. Probably bugs in the reeds, too. Nathan quickly lifted his feet to the bench, and pulled his knees tight under his chin. Where was Uncle Nevill?

He looked toward the massive, carved wood doors at the end of the hall, willing them to open and Uncle Nevill to come through. Nothing happened.

To combat his misery, Nathan studied the colorful tapestries decorating the hall. Men on horses, swords clashing, a hero standing over his conquered victim, and ladies in long, flowing gowns peopled the walls. The largest tapestry hung at the far end of the room, behind three chairs set on a low platform. It showed a fierce looking creature with outspread wings poised for flight, its red, purple and gold body shining vibrantly through the blue smoke haze.

"Look at that, Katie." Nathan dug his elbow into Katie's side. "Do you think it's a dragon?"

No answer. He turned to the girl and saw her eyes were closed. He stared at the tapestry again. A brisk gust of wind found its way through the chinks in the stone walls and the dragon rippled into menacing life. Nathan shivered. The fire might be roasting his front, but his back was freezing.

Had Uncle Nevill deserted them? It seemed like hours since he had left the room with Myrrd, promising to return shortly. Shortly, huh. He had been gone for hours and he still had a lot of explaining to do, such as where were they? How did they get here? And most importantly, could they get back?

Katie's head slumped against Nathan's arm, then immediately straightened. "Sorry," she mumbled. "Must have dozed off."

Soon Nathan felt her body lean into his again. He could understand why. He could barely keep his own eyes open, but he didn't want to fall asleep and land on those rushes. He looked at the boy sitting opposite the fire, silent and staring. Maybe he'd talk to him. He had to do something to stay awake. He couldn't remember what Uncle Nevill had called the boy.

"I'm Nathan." He pointed at his chest. "What's your name?" he asked.

The boy stared at him so long Nathan wondered if he had understood. He opened his mouth to repeat the question, when the boy suddenly spoke.

"Llien," he said.

Nathan shook his head, not understanding.

"Can you spell it?" he asked. He mimed writing with his finger. "Spell it?"

"The symbols that are my name?"

Nathan nodded. Perhaps the boy's symbols were Nathan's letters. With his foot the boy smoothed the floor before the fire. He picked up a thick reed and laboriously printed L-L-I-E-N in the gray ash.

"Llien," Nathan read.

He took a reed also and began to scratch in the ash beneath Llien's name. N-E-I-L-L.

"Neill!" Nathan cried. "Your name backwards is Neill."

Llien looked up startled, fear clouding his eyes. His fingers moved swiftly.

"What are you doing with your hand?" Nathan asked.

Llien shrugged and glanced furtively around the hall. "The sign against evil," he said.

"Evil!" Nathan caught that with no problem.

"You could be one of the nightwalkers, drawn

by the summoning. I have heard they can take on a man's form at will," Llien told him. "You could change my name and steal my soul."

Nathan's mouth hung open. He pretty much understood every word this time. Llien thought Nathan was something called a nightwalker and that was obviously not a good thing.

A pitcher materialized beneath Nathan's nose. He jumped and looked up into a rounded, unlined face. Good-natured and smiling broadly, it appeared more suited to a young child than the large man's body upon which it sat. The man/child gestured exuberantly toward their empty cups, slopping liquid from the pitcher over Llien.

"You clumsy idiot." Llien leapt from the bench and raised a fist. The man/child shrank back.

"It was only an accident." Awake now, Katie jumped to her feet. The huge man/child cowered behind her small frame. She glared at Llien, then held her cup out.

"I'll have some more."

She smiled and the man/child grinned widely, leaning forward to pour her drink. As he did so, his hair parted around his ear and Nathan saw a mark burned into the man/child's cheek, like a brand. Was he a slave?

Llien saw Nathan stare at the mark. "Yes," he said bitterly. "Even the mindtouched one has his mark."

"What do you mean?" Nathan asked.

"The mark to show his trade. He is a king's server and the brand shows him as such. Every person is born to his place, or if not born to it, soon finds his lifework. Smith, baker, warrior, farmer—you are given the mark and that is what you do."

"But what if you change your mind and want to do something different?" Katie asked.

"Once you have the mark, that is what you do," Llien said stubbornly. "If you changed, who then would do that work? It is an honor to have your mark, to know your place."

Llien's fingers stroked his cheek, then dropped away. He bent his head forward quickly so the hair would conceal the skin, but not before Nathan noticed that Llien had no mark.

"That's just plain silly," Katie argued. She plopped down on the bench.

Llien didn't reply, merely stared at her, and Nathan found himself suddenly shifting nearer the girl.

At that moment one of the carved doors opened and Uncle Nevill entered the Great Hall. He picked his way between the sleeping people to where they sat. He had changed into long robes, identical to Myrrd's in all but color, his being white shot with gold that dazzled like sunlight.

"I'm sorry to have left you alone so long," he began.

"Where are we?" Nathan interrupted.

Uncle Nevill groaned as he sat down, extending his feet before the fire. "These old bones of mine. They hate the cold."

Nathan looked at his uncle impatiently.

"Yes, Nathan," Uncle Nevill said. "The King's Counsellor and I had to confer with the King."

"What King?" Nathan interrupted again.

"If you'd let me finish you'd know," his uncle pointed out. "I am speaking of the High King of Angliocch. There are low kings, and chieftains and all manner of lesser lords governing the provinces, but the High King rules them all, and a new High King has recently ascended to the throne. Now it seems the High King's aunt, Majell, has challenged his right to do so. She sees her own son as heir." Uncle Nevill stopped, studied Llien's name written backwards in the ash and raised an eyebrow at Nathan.

"It is vital that the line of kings progress in their proper succession," he continued. "Should the order be broken, chaos will result, not only here but in your time stream as well. That is why it is imperative that Majell be defeated in this quest of hers to set her son upon the throne."

Here? But where was here? And what did Uncle Nevill mean *in your time stream as well*. Nathan shook his head irritably. Why was Uncle Nevill babbling about kings and aunts and time?

All he wanted to do was go home.

"Where are we?" Katie asked. "Did we time travel or something? Are we back in the past?"

"I'll try to explain," Uncle Nevill began. "This is not your past, nor is it your future and you know it's not your present. But it is *their* present." The man gestured around the room at the people who were sleepily getting to their feet. Fires were stirred and iron pots swung over the new flames.

"In the universe, there are time streams running parallel to each other. Separate dimensions side by side. Imagine if you will a single spring. Water bubbles up and flows, dividing itself into many channels or streams, all going their own way. So it is with the time streams. They began in one place but went in various directions; separate streams, and different people and cultures evolved along each time stream. Some primitive, even more so than this one, others more advanced."

"Like ours?" Nathan asked.

"Like yours," Uncle Nevill replied. "And beyond. The streams never cross, are independent of each other, yet they are all linked. So when something happens in one time stream, it disturbs the others, rather like a domino effect."

"But what do you have to do with this?" Nathan asked.

"I and Myrrd are keepers of the time streams,"

Uncle Nevill replied. "We are entrusted with their care. We travel the streams keeping watch and if there is trouble, do our best to keep it from getting out of hand. And that is the trick. Knowing when and when not to interfere. We try not to alter the time streams if at all possible as one change always causes another."

Nathan's mouth gaped in disbelief and Katie looked dazed, while Llien stared greedily at the old man—like a large meal had been placed before him and he was starving, but had been told he couldn't eat.

Before Nathan could ask any more questions, the hall's large wooden doors swung back and two guards shouted. "Rise! The King!"

People crowded into the Great Hall, filling it with noise. Nathan strained to see over them and finally resorted to climbing up on the bench. From here Nathan saw Myrrd make his way to the raised platform and Uncle Nevill join him, their black and the white robes contrasting like night and day.

"I don't see any king," Nathan shouted to Katie.

"My people," a high voice piped. "My people." The voice repeated and the room quieted.

Nathan craned his neck every way but could only see Uncle Nevill, the Counsellor and a scrawny kid standing between them. With one hand the boy raised a sword high above his head.

Nathan froze. He could hear the sword's song though he hadn't sought it out. It had found him. He slid deeply into its melody. It sang of being born amongst the stars, forged by magic and carried by kings. It sang of battle, pride, victory, sorrow and death, then hurtled Nathan to the top of the hill where the Nine Stones added their voice.

Standing within the ring of ancient rock, shadow figures passed before him and Nathan knew that he journeyed the time streams. Soon he reached the place of beginning; his own and that of all men and still he traveled on, toward a glowing, white light, a place beyond time. Never had he heard music like this. Each note swelled within him, agony and ecstacy intertwined. He reached out a hand eager to gather them into his being.

"Nathan! Nathan!" Katie shook his arm, her face frightened.

Nathan blinked and looked around the Great Hall. Where had he been? Or had he even left? Cheers resounded throughout the room. The boy still stood with the sword held high above his head. Slowly it dawned on Nathan. This kid was the *High King!*

Chapter 10

LLIEN STARED AT THE KING'S COUNSELLOR, SHOCK AND disappointment draining the color from his face, leaving it ashen and sickly looking.

"I am not to be WyndCaller then?" he asked. His tongue felt unfamiliar and awkward as if not belonging to him.

"No, Llien you are not," Myrrd replied. He put a hand on the boy's shoulder, but Llien pulled away.

"I am sorry," Myrrd continued. "I have done you a grievous wrong, but I had no way of knowing. You have the inborn ability to call the magic to you, that is true, but...," Myrrd's voice faltered a moment, then firmly went on. "Lately I have realized the WyndMagic would master you rather than the other way around. You do not have the strength to control it. I am sorry."

"That...that girl," Llien spat out the words. "You think she has the strength! You would make her WyndCaller!"

"I do not know yet."

"But I have seen you watch her."

"As I said—" Myrrd began.

"I have served you many years," Llien ranted.

"Waiting for the magic to be passed on to me. And now I am not to be WyndCaller! What am I to be?" Spittle flew from his mouth. "A juggler? A traveling entertainer with a few magic tricks up his sleeve?" He fiercely yanked the hair back from his cheek. "I do not bear the mark of any trade. Already people stare at me strangely, to see one my age unmarked."

"I had hoped you would stay with me," Myrrd said. "As my son."

"I do not want to be *son* of WyndCaller. I want to be *WyndCaller!*" Llien howled.

"And that is why you never will be!" Myrrd thundered. He drew himself to full height and his voice bounced off the stone walls. "You are already slave to the magic's call." He pointed a long finger at the boy's chest. "It prods and twists you in here with its need. Hurts you—"

At that moment the door swung open and Katie stood on the threshold staring from boy to man.

"I'm sorry," she apologized, and began to back from the room.

Llien pushed rudely past, throwing her a look of pure hatred. He grabbed a torch from an iron sconce on the wall and held it before him to light his way down the corridor leading to the tower. He needed to be alone and few people were willing to venture up the steep steps to the highest point of the stronghold.

As he climbed the winding stairs Llien slipped, his feet made clumsy by despair. Never had he felt such desolation. He was not to be WyndCaller. It was all he had ever dreamed of, what he had been lead to believe would be his destiny. Never had he thought to be anything else. Tears flowed down his cheeks, running salty into his mouth.

He reached the tower room and crossed to a narrow opening in the stone wall, watching a red sun rise over the distant hill of the Nine Stones. Even now this girl, Katie, was with Myrrd, receiving the training that was rightfully his. Had she never come... Llien wanted to scream his rage, but instead took deep, steadying breaths.

He rubbed a hand across his chest kneading at a tightness that lately always seemed to be with him. Only being inside WyndMagic's call eased it somewhat. He felt a momentary qualm. Was Myrrd right? Was he slave to the magic? No. He had strength enough to control it. He would prove Myrrd wrong. There were other means by which he could possess the magic.

Llien felt the constriction in his chest loosen. That was better. He needed a clear mind if he was to be WyndCaller.

Chapter 11

NATHAN LOOKED DOWN FROM HIS AND UNCLE NEVILL'S quarters into a large yard. The glass in the window was thick and poorly made, distorting the people below as if he viewed them from underwater. Men stood or squatted around warming fires, talking and laughing. Young boys and girls scurried among them ladened with pitchers and platters of food. Older youths polished shields and swords, inspected and stacked spears. Horses were led about, some calm, others skittish and nervous.

People were gathering for the young king's crowning to take place in three days time. Once this had been accomplished his uncle had promised they would go home. Wouldn't Mom be wondering where they were Nathan had asked? Uncle Nevill had assured him a slight shifting of the time stream would take care of that problem, yet not affect the others adversely.

Nathan yawned hugely, tiredness weighing down his arms and legs. He had managed a couple hours sleep but the din from outdoors had awakened him.

A watery sunbeam broke through high, thin

cloud and bounced off the glass into his eyes. It offered no warmth and Nathan shivered, feeling the cold seep in between the stone wall and wood window frame. Obviously these people had never heard of insulation.

Beneath him, Nathan saw Katie cross the yard. Squashing his nose flat against the glass, he watched as Llien joined her. Dam! Yanking a sweater over his head, Nathan ran out the door. Llien was trouble.

Clattering down stone steps, Nathan burst into the yard. He dodged past a horse's rump, and came up breathlessly beside Katie. She wore a leaf-green cloak and, Nathan saw, had traded her oversized dress for a blue gown embroidered with yellow stitching. He stared at her. He had not realized Katie's eyes were so blue, the color in the gown perfectly matching them. It fitted her well and made her look dignified—more like a girl.

She laughed at something Llien said and Nathan scowled. Obviously she had forgotten the boy's behavior the previous night. He bounced up and down trying to attract her attention, but Llien's back blocked him from her view.

"Perhaps you would do me the honor of accompanying me on a tour of Creemore Stronghold, Lady," Llien said.

Nathan looked at the other boy suspiciously.

He was being awful nice to Katie all of a sudden.
Not that there was a hope she would go with him.

Astounded, Nathan watched as Katie blushed
and nodded her head. His mouth fell open. Was
that all it took? A good-looking guy smiling and
calling her Lady and she turned to mush? Katie's
face lit up even more when Llien gallantly offered
his arm to her.

"That'd be great," Nathan said. He elbowed
his way between Katie and Llien. "What are you
going to show us?"

"The invitation is for the lady—alone," Llien
snarled.

He stalked away, pulling Katie with him, and
began to quickly weave a path through the people.
Nathan stubbornly hurried to keep up. No way
was he letting Llien get Katie alone.

The ground in the yard was slick with thawing
dirt, churned into mud by trampling feet. Nathan's
running shoes slipped and slid as he struggled to
keep Katie and Llien in sight. They passed by
stables, a smithy and kitchens, where Nathan
glanced in to see a ring of people huddled about
a stewpot, fishing for tidbits with their fingers.
He felt slightly queasy wondering if that was his
supper.

Raucous cries overhead forced Nathan's eyes
from Katie's back in time to see five crows take
sudden, noisy flight from the sloping roof of the

chapel. They glided on black wings in a wide circle above the yard, then all but one settled again on the roof. The lone bird flew off on its own. Nathan shoved his glasses up his nose and frowned. Had he seen a spot of white on the lone crow's head? At this distance it was hard to be certain and tiredness could be clouding his mind, mixing up home with Angliocch.

Llien finally stopped his whirlwind tour before a small boy who was running a sharpening stone along the blade of a sword as large as himself. Llien grabbed the weapon from the boy who protested, but backed away when Llien directed a nasty look at him. Just like Todd, Nathan realized. A born bully.

Llien examined the sword's edge with a finger, then grinned and threw it to Nathan. It fell on the ground at Nathan's feet and Llien laughed. "You are not familiar with sword play where you are from?" he asked.

"Not really," Katie answered hurriedly. "Though some people do it as a sport. Fencing."

Llien ignored her. "Pick it up," he ordered Nathan. "If you are able."

Anger surged through Nathan at the mocking tone in Llien's voice. He reached down and grabbed the sword's grip with one hand, grunted, and finally resorted to using both hands to lift it. It weighed a ton! The sword's tip wavered in the air as he struggled to hold it straight in front of him. Did people actually fight with this thing?

Llien laughed. "It's a man's weapon, and you have but a boy's strength."

He crossed to a pile of swords, selected one, and tossed it from hand to hand before nodding his approval. The small boy approached again, objecting to the plunder of his master's supplies, but ran away when Llien lunged at him with the sword.

Katie shifted nervously from foot to foot. "Perhaps we should go," she began.

Nathan was lowering the sword to the ground when he heard the air sing above him. He raised his head in time to see a silver blur arc downwards. Fear lending his arms strength, he heaved his sword up, and felt a stinging tremor race up his hands to his arms as Llien's weapon smashed into his. The blow forced him to his knees.

Katie's eyes were round with shock and, as if in slow motion, Nathan saw her arms come up. Wisps of blue snaked about her wrists and the air became ominously still. He had felt that before and knew what it meant. Katie planned to use her power. But to do what? Something horrible to Llien that she would regret all her life? He had to stop her. Llien turned to the girl, drawn by the gathering magic .

"No!" Nathan shouted. "Don't do it, Katie."

Katie's arms trembled as she struggled to rein in the magic, then dropped limply to her sides.

The few seconds of distraction had given Nathan time to stagger to his feet and raise his sword again, as Llien swung his weapon a second time. Nathan heard the sword's high, piercing killing song and gripped his weapon with numb fingers, waiting fearfully for the attack.

"Hold!"

The air vibrated with the command. Llien's sword froze in mid-swing above his head.

A woman sat tall on a white horse, her back a straight, uncompromising line. Behind her a boy sat astride a gray horse, mouth set in a permanent sneer. A burly group of men were ranged behind them. The woman pulled back her hood to release thick, black hair that fell to her waist, dramatically split by a white stripe that ran from peak to end. Nathan could not look away from the woman's beauty. She gazed at each of them in turn, a small smile playing about her lips.

Llien's arms shook under the weight of the raised sword, but he could not lower it. Sweat streaked his face. Suddenly, Nathan felt the air stir and the sword dropped, slipping from Llien's hands to fall into the mud. The boy with the woman laughed unpleasantly.

"It seems an unfair fight when one has such an advantage," the woman said. She turned her head toward Llien, black eyes studying him thoughtfully.

If the woman's beauty had any flaw, Nathan saw, it was her nose, too narrow and long, beak-like. Without thinking he listened, searching for the woman's song. Gasping, he stepped back as her face suddenly withered and became lined like that of an old woman, then abruptly smoothed and glowed with youth and beauty once more. So swiftly had the change taken place that Nathan wondered if his eyes were playing tricks on him. Then he found her song and appearance was forgotten.

Weaving through the woman's song was the ancient melody he'd found in Uncle Nevill's and the Nine Stone's songs. Except hers sounded wrong; distorted and twisted into something dark and evil.

Sudden pain ripped through Nathan's head, as if a fist had slammed into his mind. Through tear-filled eyes, Nathan saw the woman smile at him. She had done that. She had felt his probing and had easily, casually, entered his mind. Nathan knew then that she was one of those his uncle had warned him about. One who would leave him without a mind.

The woman appeared to lose interest in him and prodded her horse forward a couple of paces toward Katie. The girl's face paled until only her eyes, deep pools of blue, held color.

Nathan! Pain jolted through Nathan's aching head. Katie had somehow linked to his mind! She needed his help.

He tried to reach her, but his feet would not move. Horrified Nathan watched as his toes sprouted brown, gnarled roots that burrowed deep into the earth holding him fast. His legs melded together taking on the rough bark of a tree trunk.

"Majell. Balddrick. What brings you here?" Uncle Nevill strode past the woman's horse and put a hand on Katie's shoulder.

Nathan saw the girl slump forward. He could *hear* singing in his mind and realized it was Uncle Nevill assuring him he had not become a tree. Nathan looked down to see his running shoes, roots gone.

"I have come to see that things are well with my nephew," the woman said. "I do worry about him so."

Nathan clearly heard the lie beneath the seemingly kind words. Should he warn Uncle Nevill? *I hear!* sang Uncle Nevill again. Why was he suddenly hearing everyone in his mind, Nathan wondered?

"The King's aunt and cousin should have a proper escort," his uncle said. He gestured and a small company of armed soldiers rode up behind Majell's band of men and Uncle Nevill led the way to the yard.

Nathan trailed behind, tugging a disoriented Katie with him. Llien had disappeared. Probably scared, Nathan thought disgustedly, worried about protecting his own skin.

Katie stumbled and Nathan quickly put a hand under her arm, only to find the man/child servant already there steadying the girl.

"Katie? Are you okay?" Nathan asked.

She didn't answer, merely gazed at him with unfocused eyes. Nathan didn't know what to do. He could try to find her song. He might be able to help her that way. But he wanted to forget about *hearing* and *songs*. It scared him. Look what had happened when he had listened to Majell. She could have blown his brain apart. Better he leave Katie's care to Uncle Nevill. But why, Nathan wondered, did his decision leave him feeling so miserable?

At the entrance to the Great Hall, the High King and his Counsellor waited, a large crowd gathered before them. Upon seeing his aunt the boy looked scared and very young, then straightened his shoulders.

"Well come, Aunt. Cousin," he said calmly.

Majell slid from her horse and stood waiting, but the boy made no move to invite her into the hall. She would have to speak in front of everyone.

"I have come to ask you to reconsider your position," Majell began. "You are young and inexperienced. This is well known in the far holdings and they will soon send armies to test your strength. I ask that you think of your people and your land before you let stubborn pride cause unnecessary blood to be spilt.

"My own son is older," she continued, "and has been well trained in leadership. I ask only that he rule for a short time, until you have grown. I do not ask that you give up your kingship, only that you allow my son to act as your regent, until you are able to rule in your own right."

She could have something there, Nathan thought. A puny kid like this couldn't possibly rule a country.

"It is a solution your father, my beloved brother," Majell's voice broke slightly, "would have approved of."

All around him Nathan could hear men muttering and nodding their heads in agreement. It made pretty good sense. The woman was only doing her duty, doing what she thought best for the land and its people. Even the king looked uncertain. Nathan rubbed his forehead. His mind worked sluggishly, like someone had packed his brain with cotton balls.

"And when it came time to return the crown, what then, Majell?" Myrrd asked, his voice echoing through the yard.

"Would you ever consider him ready to rule

or perhaps he would come down with a mysterious, deadly ailment, such as that which claimed his father. You would soon have people forgetting there was ever any king save your son."

Nathan felt like a bucket of cold water had been thrown on him, instantly clearing his mind. He looked at the woman standing before the boy king and could hear that she spoke nothing but lies. How had she made him believe otherwise? Others in the yard had believed her, too. Even the High King looked like he had been rudely awakened.

"Such beguiling words, Aunt," the King said angrily. "*I* am High King. And I will have your pledge." The words rang from the boy's lips and Nathan realized that royal blood indeed ran through the kid's veins.

Red stained Majell's face as she swung on to her horse. She kneed the animal forward, bent down and handed the boy a black crow's feather.

"The war feather!" a man behind Nathan exclaimed.

"One day I will give for your preparations, then we meet on the battlefield." Majell wheeled her horse around and the crowd parted silently, allowing her passage. She turned her head only once—to stare at Katie.

"My people!" The boy's voice broke the silence.

He drew his sword from its jeweled scabbard
and raised it high above his head to point skyward.
Nathan gaped. How on earth could that skinny
kid lift that thing? And with one hand? He knew
from experience how much those swords
weighed.

"We go into battle!"

Chapter 12

LLIEN CAUTIOUSLY PARTED THE TANGLE OF VINES AND brush and wriggled his body through the opening, cursing silently as thorns tore his clothing and skin. He had hidden in the thicket at the bottom of the hill most of the afternoon, waiting for night. From his hiding place he had watched the excitement and chaos the black war feather had wrought. Watched men riding to and fro along the dirt road leading to the stronghold, their faces as grim as the messages they carried. Then the first wagons had arrived, wooden wheels groaning beneath their cargo of people and supplies.

To Llien's dismay, a watchguard had been posted on the road, so he was unable to move from his cramped hiding place for fear of being seen. Leg muscles knotted painfully and his feet were numb by the time night fell.

Finally, the road quieted and the guard settled beside the warmth of the sentinel fire. Llien paused to listen, but hearing no sound continued to worm his way through the thicket. Breaking free of it, he crept noiselessly past the guard's back and fled down the road away from the stronghold.

Cold and tired he sorely longed for a warm bed, but Majell had beckoned him and he had no choice but to go. Not that he minded the meeting. His own clumsy attempts to get rid of the girl had failed. That boy, Nathan, had come along and ruined things. With Majell's help, perhaps he would be more successful in disposing of Katie, leaving only himself to be WyndCaller.

Nerves taut, Llien walked rapidly, uncomfortably aware of faint rustlings from behind the forest wall. He did not know which he feared more, man or animal, or those that were neither. His fingers moved rapidly in the evil warding sign and he pulled his cloak tight about him, but couldn't still his shivering.

The forest ended, and rocky, barren land took over. Llien left the road and stumbled over uneven ground to where a stand of oaks stood out starkly black in the flat field. He passed a horse, hobbled, head down nibbling sparse fare, then walked beneath the first of the enormous oaks. He stopped then, reluctant to go further into their dark reaches.

Suddenly, Majell materialized out of the shadows, the white streak in her black hair shining silver in the moon's thin light. Llien bowed his head and dropped to one knee, gestures normally reserved for royalty. His heart pounded loud in his ears.

"You may rise," she said generously, well pleased with him.

He felt her then inside his mind, probing. He tried to repel her and then attempted to conceal his thoughts, but found he could do neither.

"Such ambitions," Majell said, greatly amused. "I could help you achieve them, if you wish."

For a moment Llien hesitated, afraid of giving himself so totally to her and feeling, unexpectedly, a pang of loyalty toward Myrrd that made him hold his tongue. The dull ache in his chest sharpened until he could barely breathe. Then the anticipation of owning and wielding WyndMagic pushed away the uncertainty and he quickly nodded.

"Well, then, I have a plan," Majell told him. "I would caution you, boy, that I do not accept failure."

Llien licked his suddenly dry lips and bent his head forward to listen carefully to Majell.

Chapter 13

NATHAN STOOD ON THE PLATFORM OF THE WOODEN palisade and stared out at the blackness before him. Like stars sprinkling a night sky the yellow campfires of Majell's armies dotted the wide plain far below. Creemore Stronghold itself was filled to overflowing with warriors loyal to the High King. Hearing footsteps on the ladder behind him, Nathan turned to see Uncle Nevill's head, then his body, rise up the side of the platform.

"I'm taking a much needed break from all that war talk," his uncle said. He joined Nathan and looked out over the plain, slowly shaking his head. "Majell must have planned this for months. And promised generous settlements of land to have assembled such a vast army."

Seeing Nathan's puzzled look he explained. "Majell's supporters are chieftains with holdings in the north country. It's rocky, unproductive land and they eke out a meagre existence. Long have the north people looked greedily to the fertile soils of the south. They see this as their opportunity, I suppose."

"Who exactly is Majell?" Nathan asked.

There was a long silence. "She is the King's aunt," Uncle Nevill said finally, then added, "once she was one of us."

"One of us?" Nathan repeated.

"A Keeper of the time streams." His uncle sighed deeply. "We were three, Myrrd, Majell and myself. Three entrusted to care for the time streams. Things ran smoothly for a long while, then Majell became restless. She'd had a taste of power and no longer wanted to be bound by Keepers' rules. Sometimes power does that, finds a weakness, a flaw in a person that it can worm its way into and force wider."

"So Majell went off on her own. Myrrd and I managed to place some restrictions on her. She cannot cross the time streams in human form, which is good as she cannot work her magic in any form but human. Still, she is capable of wreaking much havoc."

Not cross the time streams in human form! Nathan's mind reeled.

Uncle Nevill smiled at his horrified look. "Majell is a ShapeChanger," he explained. "She can be any living thing she chooses; animal, bird, fish, person, and she can make you believe anything she wants, can bend your mind."

"Can she be a...a crow?" Nathan stammered.

"Hmmm...you have noticed that, too," Uncle Nevill commented.

Nathan thought for a moment then asked, "Is Myrrd really Merlin?"

"He has so many names I often lose track of them." Uncle Nevill shrugged. "Perhaps Merlin is one."

"Llien said Myrrd was a WyndCaller," Nathan said.

"Myrrd has the ability to call the power of the wind to him," Uncle Nevill explained. "And through it can draw upon the other elements— earth, fire, water—for their magic. A WyndCaller."

"That's what Katie can do," Nathan interrupted. "Does that mean she is a WyndCaller too?"

"She has the ability. But it remains to be seen if she has the strength to control the WyndMagic. It tends to want to do all the controlling itself." Uncle Nevill fell silent, leaning forward again to study the armies below.

"And...," Nathan prompted.

"And what?"

"You. What kind of magic can you do?"

"I can see into your heart," Uncle Nevill said. "I am a TruthSinger." He leaned over and tapped a bent finger on Nathan's chest. "Through my music I know what's really in here. No matter what the disguise, what the deceit, I see truth."

Nathan felt like a balloon rapidly deflating. A TruthSinger! Big deal! What was that compared to changing yourself into a bear or lion, or causing it to thunder whenever you wanted. But to know the truth—heck, even he could do that. Could tell Todd was a bully, Llien too. Could *hear* the goodness in Katie despite it being buried beneath layers of distrust and fear.

Even he could do that! Nathan's eyes widened. Did that mean...? He whirled around, but Uncle Nevill was gone.

Nathan slowly turned back to stare into the night. He felt trapped, as if a net was slowly closing about him and he couldn't escape. What if this Majell lady won? What would happen to him and Katie? Would they be stuck here forever? Nathan shuddered remembering the way Majell had looked at Katie, like she was studying a bug stuck on the sharp end of a pin.

A finger suddenly tapped his shoulder and Nathan jumped, heart thudding.

"Sorry," Katie said. "I didn't mean to scare you. I guess you didn't hear us coming up the ladder."

"Uh...no, I didn't," Nathan stammered. Us?

Behind Katie stood a second figure—the kid king.

"This is the High King of Angliocch," Katie said grandly.

The boy groaned and rolled his eyes. "Call me Tegarron," he said to Nathan.

Nathan didn't know what he was supposed to do; bow, curtsy—nah, girls did that. He stuck out his hand. "Pleased to meet you."

From the corner of his eye, Nathan saw the ladder swing away from the platform, hang suspended in mid-air a moment, then fall from view. The *thump* caused the platform to quiver as if a large tree had been felled nearby. The three of them rushed to the edge and peered over.

A body lay sprawled in the dirt below. Upon seeing them a mud-caked face broke into a huge grin—the man/child servant.

"Brull. Are you all right?" Katie asked anxiously. She waited until the big head nodded vigorously, then turned to Nathan and Tegarron. "He's kind of attached himself to me," she said sheepishly.

Tegarron laughed and leaned back against the palisade, spinning a gold circlet on one finger. It splashed the wood walls and floor with flecks of yellow light. "Nevill tells me you crossed the time streams with him," he said.

Katie and Nathan exchanged startled looks.

"Yes, I know about the time streams," the boy assured them. "I have difficulty grasping the reality of them, how they work and the fact there are different worlds in each. Still it must be an exciting adventure to travel from one time to another," he finished wistfully.

An adventure! Nathan felt stunned. This kid was a king, was threatened with death by his aunt, commanded armies about to go into battle and still—he wished for an exciting adventure!

"How did you lift that sword so easily?" Nathan blurted out.

The boy seemed surprised by the question, but no more so than Nathan. He hadn't meant to speak out loud. He'd just been thinking about battles and fighting.

"My sword has been spelled by Myrrd. Good thing, too. It is far too heavy for my skinny arms." Tegarron comically flexed his biceps. "Myrrd assures me I'll soon grow, but for now says I shouldn't be ashamed of a little outside help." He bent his head toward them. "But I'll expect you to keep my secret."

"Your Majesty!"

They craned their necks over the side of the platform once again and this time saw a man frowning up at them, face rigid with disapproval. Nathan saw the eager boyishness wiped from Tegarron's face, replaced by a weariness that sat strangely old on the smooth skin. He studied the High King. He couldn't be more than nine or ten years old, but had he ever been allowed to be just a kid?

"Your Majesty," the man repeated. "Your presence is required in the council chambers."

"Very well," Tegarron said resignedly.

Brull scrambled to put the ladder in place.

"Makes him mad." Tegarron gestured to the man below, keeping his voice quiet so only Nathan and Katie could hear. "Been my guardian all my life and still can't figure out how I get away from him. Years ago Father showed me a secret passage from the royal quarters to outside. Forget jewels or crowns. It's the most valuable asset I have."

Brull lumbered up the ladder and jumped exuberantly onto the platform, making it tremble until Nathan feared it would break. The servant bowed so low to Tegarron his forehead scraped the floor.

"I see Brull attends you. No one could take better care of you than he," Tegarron said kindly.

Brull beamed, basking in the warm praise.

With a final smile the boy scrambled down the ladder and Nathan unexpectedly found himself bowing to the High King of Angliocch.

"He's nice," Katie said. She stood on tiptoe and peered over the wooden wall. "Hard to believe that this will be a battlefield in the morning. Tegarron was telling me that the whole war takes place right here. The armies from each side meet in the middle and fight it out. It's all organized in advance. No smart bombs or missiles." She smiled wanly.

"Where've you been?" Nathan asked. "I looked for you all afternoon."

"Well, first of all I was talking to Myrrd, then I was with Tegarron listening to the battle plans in the royal chambers."

Great! He'd been worried sick about her and she'd been having the time of her life, hanging out with WyndCallers and kings.

"Myrrd was explaining to me about WyndMagic," Katie said, unaware of Nathan's simmering anger. "I was so scared you know, because I could do these things—think about something and it would come true. I was so scared I would hurt someone. Myrrd says that won't happen because it isn't in me to cause hurt. Myrrd says it's possible I might be a WyndCaller, too." She tried to sound casual, but Nathan could hear the excitement in her voice.

"Myrrd says it's quite a responsibility. Everytime you use the WyndMagic, the power has to be taken from somewhere else. It leaves an imbalance. Remember when I made you float over the ice, then that windstorm came up? Myrrd says it was a reaction to my using WyndMagic. Myrrd says you have to carefully weigh everything you do before you do it to see if the consequences bear out the action. Myrrd says he'll teach me how to control the magic once this war is taken care of."

Myrrd says...Myrrd says...Was she going to parrot the man all night long? He hated what was happening here, what was happening to her. Everything was spinning out of control.

"I want us to go home," Nathan announced.

"Why?" Katie looked surprised.

"I just think its time *we* went home. We don't belong here. It's not our time."

"I like this place," Katie said.

"But you don't belong here," Nathan repeated.

"How do you know where I belong?" Katie asked angrily. "It sure beats what's waiting for me in our time stream. Look at my life there— my house, walking around on eggshells all the time, keeping out of Dad's way, Mom exhausted, no money, second hand clothes that don't fit." She stroked the blue gown. "Back home I'm weird. People don't like me and I don't like them. Here I'm special and it's nice." Her voice pleaded for him to understand but Nathan's misery left no room for sympathy.

"And then there's Llien," he said.

"What do you mean?"

"Oh, come on! He smiles at you and you turn all—" Nathan groped for the right word. "All girl!"

"All girl," Katie echoed disgustedly. "Here's a newsflash for you—I am a girl. You're so stupid. I only acted that way because I knew Llien was up to no good. I was hoping to find out what his plans were, but you came along and messed up everything."

"I was trying to protect you," Nathan declared.

"I don't need protecting. I am perfectly capable of taking care of myself and, in case you hadn't noticed, of you, too. I have magic, you know."

"Fine!" Nathan shouted. "Stay here if you want."

Brull moved forward to stand between them, glowering at Nathan.

"Guess he thinks I need protecting too," Katie said. She stalked to the end of the platform.

Nathan glared at the bulky servant blocking his way, then flopped down and hung his head between his knees. Dam! He was in a terrible mood. M-O-O-D D-O-O-M DOOM! Omigosh! Was that some kind of omen? Were they all doomed? He was driving himself crazy.

"Brull," Nathan said. "Brull. Your name backwards is LLURB."

Brull stared at him, face blank.

"See," Nathan explained. "Your name is Brull. Now say it backwards and it's Llurb. LLURB," he repeated loudly.

"You don't have to yell at him. He's not deaf," Katie pointed out. "He doesn't understand what you mean. Few people would." Her voice trailed off as she stepped forward into the torchlight.

"You know," she said softly. "You have magic, too, inside. I can..." She stopped, searching for the right words. "I can *feel* it in you," she said slowly. "...and it's all wrapped up in...your music." She looked directly at him. "But you keep pushing the magic away."

She stared at him a moment longer, then bunched her skirt above her knees and climbed down the ladder. Brull immediately followed.

Pushing the magic away... Nathan shoved his glasses up his nose. What did she know about music and *hearing* and Dad not wanting him. Magic was a curse!

A blast of cold air sent shivers up his back. Dam! He'd been freezing his butt off since he'd arrived here. This wasn't his home, or his battle, or his time stream. He'd had enough.

He stomped down the ladder. You have magic, too, inside.... Well, too bad. It would just have to stay there, inside. He'd made his choice and music wasn't it. He headed across the yard toward the stronghold to find Uncle Nevill.

Chapter 14

SQUEEZING HIS WAY PAST A SMALL GIRL PETTING A bleating goat, Nathan flung himself down on a bench beside Uncle Nevill. It was hot in the Great Hall, the air a solid wall of stench. His head throbbed from the incredible uproar. It appeared that every farmer and herdsman under the king's protection had brought family and livestock to the stronghold for protection. A servant girl pressed a cup of the ever present sweet-sour ale into Nathan's hands. He looked at it dubiously, then took a mouthful, grimacing as he swallowed. Another reason why he hated it here.

"Not to your liking?" Uncle Nevill laughed.

"When am I going home?" Nathan asked bluntly. "You can get me home, right?"

"Oh yes," Uncle Nevill assured him. "Or rather, Myrrd can. I'm afraid it's not my strength to move people from stream to stream. That's Myrrd's doing. But right now he needs all his energy for the battle tomorrow."

A moth-eaten dog sniffed at Nathan's leg. He tucked his foot beneath the bench but the animal persisted.

"You said 'I'," Uncle Nevill continued. "Is Katie not returning with you?"

"I don't know," Nathan replied. Why did he feel so glum? G-L-U-M M-U-L-G. MULG. You'd think he'd be happy to see the last of her; so pesky and irritating. But instead he felt MULG.

"She likes it here, she says." He shoved the dog away, but it came right back.

"Well, she's had a hard time back home, I imagine she would feel happier here," Uncle Nevill said.

"Guess so. Besides, she's pretty important now that she can do magic and all." Dam dog!

"Is she?" Uncle Nevill's eyebrows arched high and a thoughtful look crossed his face, then cleared as he studied Nathan.

"You are out of sorts, boy," he said, "because you aren't being true to yourself. At the moment you are a round peg trying desperately to fit into a square hole."

Nathan squirmed impatiently. He hated preaching.

"Music is as vital to you as breathing."

"It's not anything great," Nathan said sullenly. "Not like hitting a home run, or scoring a goal. It's just music."

"Music is the one constant that embraces all the time streams," Uncle Nevill told him. "Tone, rhythm, song—people everywhere understand

and need music. Food and drink might feed the body, but music feeds the soul. It is an extremely powerful force.

"Music can lift these people's spirits." Uncle Nevill gestured around the room. "Lighten their daily burden, ease their grief and hardship. Music can lead men to courage in battle—and to love. Tell me, Nathan, have you ever *listened* to your own song?"

Nathan sat perfectly still. It had never occurred to him that he might have a song. Yet it was as obvious as the nose on his face. He gnawed a fingernail. Did he really want to listen to his own song? What if he didn't like what he found there?

Taking a deep breath, he closed his eyes and blocked the din of the hall from his mind, turning his listening inward. He could hear it! *Hear* his own song! His first delight rapidly faded as feelings of cowardice and fear flooded him. Omigosh! Dad was right. He was a first class wimp! He wanted to leave then, escape the pain of listening.

Deeper! a voice commanded, and reluctantly Nathan slid back into his song and this time heard courage waiting for him, needing only to be found. Quickly peeling away layer after layer, Nathan explored his song, until he unexpectedly came upon the glowing, white light; the place beyond time that the sword's song had led him to.

Frightened, he surfaced abruptly. Why would his song be connected to the sword's?

"Bard!" A voice called from the front of the hall. "Will you sing for us before we go into battle?"

Uncle Nevill nodded his head and stood to make his way to the front of the Great Hall. Suddenly he leaned over and tapped Nathan on the shoulder. "Some time soon you will have to decide. You won't always croak, boy," he whispered. "But do hurry and find your voice, for I grow weary."

Nathan left the Great Hall and headed to his quarters. He wanted to be alone—to think about round pegs and square holes.

He approached the hallway leading past the council chambers and noticed the torches had been extinguished, recently, for most still sent up curls of blue smoke. Smoke—or mist? Nathan felt a moment's alarm, then told himself not to be stupid. Someone had put out the torches. So what?

He remained standing, reluctant to enter the blackened corridor and suddenly thought he glimpsed movement in the darkness before him. He scrunched his glasses up his nose, reluctant to go down the corridor. He could listen, he told himself, just for a moment to see if it was safe. As long as he didn't make a habit of doing it.

Listening, Nathan found a thin thread of the magic's ancient song wending its way down the hall. He could also hear someone walking stealthily in the darkness before him, though he couldn't tell who. Magic concealed the user.

Nathan peered anxiously down the passageway. Someone was using magic. He was no match for magic. He should leave, find Uncle Nevill or Myrrd, but suddenly his feet carried him down the corridor. He reached up and pried a smouldering torch from its holder and swung it from side to side. A poor weapon against magic, but better than nothing.

Hugging the wall, Nathan ran one hand along the rough stone to guide his way. In the darkness ahead a door opened and shut. He stood motionless, heart thumping. This was so dam stupid. DIPUTS! Air stirred gently about Nathan's face, then stilled. Someone had passed by him. He listened, but couldn't find the magic's song anywhere. Or the user.

Nathan retraced his steps down the passageway and into the Great Hall where he heard a lingering trace of the magic's song. Stepping over a sleeping warrior, Nathan saw one of the giant doors at the end of the hall open, then silently close. Throwing caution aside, Nathan ran to the door and pulled it wide, in time to see a figure slip through the stronghold's gate.

Concealing-spell discarded, the figure's face was momentarily illuminated by moonlight. Llien! He cradled a long cloth-wrapped bundle in his arms.

Nathan hopped from foot to foot. He should tell Uncle Nevill, Myrrd, Katie! Alert the guard! Instead he raced through the gate after the boy.

Bitter cold seared his throat as Nathan struggled to keep Llien in view. Weeds and grass glistened with silver frost that crunched beneath his feet. Llien walked rapidly down the road leading from the stronghold through dense wood, still clutching his burden. Nathan darted from tree to bush fearful of being seen, but Llien did not look back. Clouds raced dark across a waxing moon, bathing the dirt road with blue white light, then plunging it into black shadow. With each step away from the stronghold, Nathan became more alarmed. Where were they going?

Suddenly, Llien vanished into a heavily treed area at the side of the road. Nathan raced up and down trying to find the place where Llien had entered the forest. He finally saw the narrow opening and rushed in.

The woods bordering the road were dense, allowing little light through their branch canopy. Nathan staggered aimlessly about, confused and panicky. Suddenly, a small yellow light shone in front of him and he gratefully stumbled toward it, but, upon reaching the place where it had been, found the light had moved further ahead. Needle-sharp thorns tore his skin and coat as he followed the beckoning light deeper into the forest. A whisper breathed across his ear and gray shadows ringed him. Soft, ghost fingers caressed his face. Terrified, Nathan realized the light was enthraling him! He had to fight it now, before it lured him so far into the woods he'd never find his way back.

Intent on escaping the bewitching light, Nathan began to run, not stopping until a jutting root tripped him and ended his headlong flight. He lay panting on the ground, feeling warm blood flow from a cut knee. This was no good. He would only hurt himself charging around like this. Best that he stay in one spot and wait until morning.

He sat against a wide trunk and drew his knees up to his chin for warmth. Images of yellow eyes on the hillside of the Nine Stones haunted him. Did those eyes hunt in packs? Did they rip out your throat or just start gnawing on whatever limb was handy?

He'd botched it. Lost Llien and lost himself. Now he'd never find out what Llien had stolen from the stronghold. He wished Katie was around to save him. He hated to admit it, but he relied upon her coming to his rescue. He'd miss her when he went home—alone.

He leaned back against the tree, body trembling violently from fear and cold. Where was all that courage he'd heard earlier in his song? Nathan buried his head beneath his arms, fighting a memory that refused to leave him. He feared it more than the terrifying white light or even the woods. For he had been shown his need for music. A need that he now knew would always possess him. No escape. With that last thought his body slumped forward in exhausted sleep.

Nathan's head hit the ground with a *thunk*. He woke abruptly and jumped to his feet, spinning anxiously in a wide circle. There was nothing there. Dam! He'd actually fallen asleep. Dinner all served up, ready and waiting for some hungry animal.

The hard, gray light of dawn forced its way through the upper branches of the forest. Nathan saw the road not twenty steps from where he stood. He'd been running in circles! Suddenly, he heard shouting and loud voices.

Dropping to his hands and knees, Nathan crawled to the edge of the road and peered out from behind a screen of brush. Men ran every which way carrying spears and bows. Others rode foam-flecked horses at high speeds, hooves pounding on the road. The battle! It had started!

Nathan rolled over on his back plucking dead leaves from his chest. How could he get past those men and back to the stronghold? One look at his blue jeans and running shoes and they'd know he wasn't one of them. And it didn't take a rocket scientist to figure out that if you weren't one of them, you were the enemy.

He frowned, teeth gnawing at a fingernail. Strange, but he could no longer see the top of the trees, and now—their trunks had vanished! Like a woolly, white blanket, thick mist shrouded the trees. Soon, Nathan could see nothing, and, he realized, if he couldn't see—neither could anyone else.

Nathan carefully ran by the side of the road. Ghost figures floated out of the thick murk and as quickly disappeared, but no one stopped or questioned him. Never had he seen such a fog. It caught in his throat and reeked of magic, but who's—Myrrd's or Majell's?

Nathan's legs ached and his side knotted in a sharp stitch. He had been running forever. He must have passed Creemore Stronghold in the fog. Suddenly, he crashed into a wooden wall. A hand grabbed his upper arm and a face was thrust into his. Nathan tried to pull away from the stink of sour breath and stale sweat, but the guard held him firmly. Finally the man grunted and pushed him away toward the stronghold. Welcome home, Nathan thought wryly.

He hurried across the yard toward the Great Hall. It was imperative that he tell Uncle Nevill about Llien using magic and stealing from the stronghold. As he passed through the wooden doors his arm was gripped again. Nathan looked up to see Brull looming over him, worry marring his normally cheerful face.

"Eeeninsenotssss," Brull hissed.

"What?" Nathan asked impatiently.

"EEENINSENOTSSS," Brull repeated.

"Brull. I don't have time for your nonsense right now." Nathan tore his arm away from Brull's grasp.

Brull's hand flailed at empty air as he tried to reach Nathan again. "LLURB! LLURB!" he cried.

Nathan ignored him. He ran to the passageway leading to the council chambers. Fighting his way through men in battle dress, Nathan gawked at the muscled, stout bodies moving effortlessly beneath the heavy weight of leather armor and iron weapons.

Squirming beneath a massive arm as thick as a tree trunk he pushed his way into the council chambers and saw Uncle Nevill, face dark with anger, arguing with a man Nathan recognized as Tegarron's guardian.

"Uncle Nevill! Uncle Nevill!" Nathan called urgently. Upon seeing him, the elderly man crossed the room quickly, grabbed Nathan's arm and gave it a shake. Nathan winced. He'd be black and blue by tomorrow.

"I've been looking for you, boy. You and Katie both disappearing during a battle. I'd think you'd have more sense than to worry me at a time like this," Uncle Nevill scolded furiously. "And now I learn the High King is missing too."

"Uncle Nevill, listen. I have something important to tell you," Nathan pleaded. He stopped abruptly, seeing Llien standing across from him, a smug smile curving his lips.

"Well, what is it? I must get back." Uncle Nevill's eyes wandered to a group of men clustered about Myrrd.

"Um...um...," Nathan stammered. He couldn't tell Uncle Nevill about Llien now. The boy would just deny everything and Uncle Nevill was already mad and would never believe Nathan. "Umm...there's a thick fog outside," he said.

"I know there's a thick fog outside," Uncle Nevill repeated impatiently. "Myrrd put it there to confuse the armies. To buy us some time. We're trying to settle this war without bloodshed if possible. Now if that is all...?"

Nathan found himself alone.

"How was your night in the woods?" Llien sidled up beside him and grinned.

He had known, Nathan realized. Llien had known the whole time that Nathan was following him and had led him on a wild goose chase.

"You won't get away with it," Nathan said

angrily. "Whatever you're up to."

"Oh, but I already have." Llien leaned forward and shoved Nathan. "And there is nothing you can do to stop me."

A blue spark crackled on the air between the two boys. Llien drew back in surprise. "You? You possess magic too?" he asked incredulously, then laughed. "It will do you no good."

Nathan pushed past Llien and stalked out of the room, trying not to show how unnerved he was.

"EENINSENOTSSS." A hand clawed at his arm.

"Brull, quit with the gibberish would you." Nathan pushed passed the man/child, but Brull followed plucking at his back with a meaty hand.

"Stop doing that!" Nathan yelled. Then abruptly stopped. Brull plowed into him, but Nathan barely noticed. Something Uncle Nevill had said...Katie and the High King were missing!

"Brull, do you know where Katie is?" Nathan asked.

"ENIN SENOTS," Brull repeated slowly.

Nathan threw his hands up in disgust and stomped down the passageway. ENIN SENOTS! ENIN SENOTS! He'd never get any sense out of Brull.

He passed through the Great Hall into the kitchen. Maybe he'd feel better with something in his stomach. Grabbing a loaf of bread, he began hacking off a thick chunk, when suddenly the knife clattered onto the tabletop.

ENIN SENOTS. ENIN SENOTS! *NINE STONES!*

That's what Brull had tried to tell him. Katie had given the servant a backwords message.

Nathan raced out of the kitchen, across the yard and through the gate. He heard a yell behind him but kept running. Katie was at the Nine Stones.

Chapter 15

BREATHING HARD, NATHAN SCRAMBLED UP THE MUD-
slick path to the flat hilltop. The Nine Stones rose
above him, their ancient rock washed a fiery red
by the setting sun. *Setting sun?* It was only mid-
morning by Nathan's figuring. The false sunset
must be a reaction to Myrrd using WyndMagic to
create the fog.

Warriors ringed the stones, sword blades
catching and throwing red shafts of light. Above
their heads flew the standard of Majell's personal
guard. They faced inward, looking away from
Nathan, intent upon something taking place
within the circle. Dam! This was so DIPUTS! He
couldn't take on Majell's whole army! But Katie
had sent that message. For once she needed *him!*

He crouched over and ran toward the Nine
Stones, feet stumbling over the trampled ground.
Not a tree or bush grew to offer him cover. At
any minute Nathan expected to feel the piercing
thrust of a sword or spear. Nearing the circle of
warriors, he dropped flat on his stomach and
inched his way forward. Prickly weeds stabbed
his palms and fingers but he was too amazed to

notice. No one had glanced his way! Not even once. Something very interesting must be going on.

He rolled into a shallow hollow and poked his head over its slight rise. The last dying rays of the false sunset streaked the sky with violet, and gray twilight softened the warriors into shadowy spectres. He saw a space between two of Majell's men, wide enough to allow him to sneak through unseen.

Nathan jumped to his feet and sprinted, sliding to a skin peeling stop behind one of the Nine Stones. A steal, he thought smugly, of which any base runner would be proud. He caught his breath a moment, then peered around the side of the stone, careful to keep his body away from the rock.

Within the ring of the Nine Stones he could see two figures circling each other, though the smaller of them staggered about dazedly. This figure was also washed in red, coloring Nathan at first thought came from the setting sun, then remembered seeing the crimson globe sink below the horizon. It was blood! Nathan stared at the boy. The High King's blood!

The second figure Nathan now recognized as Balddrick, Majell's son. The boy raised his sword above his head and swung it downward at the High King. Tegarron struggled to lift his weapon with two hands. He managed to stop the blow from splitting his skull, but went sprawling on his back in the dirt. Why, Nathan wondered, was Tegarron having so much difficulty handling his sword? Hadn't Myrrd used magic to make it weightless?

He chomped at a ragged fingernail. The first thing he had to do was find Katie. She could use her WyndMagic to help Tegarron. He looked anxiously around the circle but couldn't see her in the gathering gloom. The longer he stayed here, the greater were his chances of being found.

As night deepened torches were lit, sending giant, flickering shadows across the circle. Finally Nathan saw Katie standing across from him, calmly watching the fight, face frozen in a familiar stillness. It had been a long time since he had seen her looking stone-like. Majell suddenly appeared beside the girl. Nathan drew back into the shadow of the stone. Katie was Majell's prisoner!

Nathan's legs trembled as he remembered Majell forcing her way into his mind. She was too strong for him. He'd have to return to the stronghold and get help. He looked back at the two boys in the circle.

The High King lay in the dirt where he had fallen. Balddrick pranced about him, pretending to stab, then drawing away, cruelly prolonging his certain victory. Tegarron wouldn't last much longer, Nathan knew. There was no time to get help. He'd have to decide and decide quickly.

His only strength was *listening*. And he didn't want to do that. Was scared to *hear* the sword's song linked so closely to his own. He didn't want to be part of all this magic stuff. Thoughts skidded and collided in his mind: *want to please Dad...want things back the way they were...round peg in a square hole...the line of kings must progress in their proper succession...music...loved music.* And that, he suddenly realized, was what it all came down to—he loved music. He knew what to do. With the decision came calmness and resolve.

Nathan watched Balddrick swing his sword in wide arcs over Tegarron. He didn't appear to be having any problems with his weapon. A sudden image of Llien hurrying through the stronghold's gates with a long, narrow burden flashed into Nathan's mind. He directed his listening to the sword in Tegarron's hand. Nothing. Not even a hint of magic. He extended his listening to the other boy and this time heard the familiar song of the High King's sword. No wonder Balddrick fought so easily—he had Tegarron's sword!

Suddenly a body crashed into Nathan, carrying him forwards away from the stone. His glasses flew from his face. He struggled to free himself from the heavy weight on top of his back. Todd! No—Todd wasn't here. With a mighty twist, he spun his body around to see Llien's grinning face hovering above him. Rage coursed through Nathan. He was tired of people picking on him.

His arms were pinned down, but Nathan discovered his feet were free. He'd once seen a wrestling show on television, where one hulk had put his foot in the stomach of the other and kicked the man up and over his head. He had practiced the move on a sofa cushion, but would it work on a real live person?

Grunting, he swung his foot up and kicked. Llien immediately groaned and rolled off Nathan. He lay moaning on the ground. Nathan scrambled for his glasses, put them on his nose and studied Llien. Waves of embarassment swept over him. He'd been aiming for Llien's stomach. He hadn't meant to get him *there!* Still, he'd better do something before Llien recovered.

He grabbed Llien's arm and wrapped it around the stone nearest him. Nathan's stomach heaved as he watched the mottled gray hardness creep up Llien's arm as the stone responded to the magic in the boy. Seeing Llien firmly attached, Nathan climbed to his feet.

Now all he had to do was free Katie and Tegarron. All he had to do...Nathan directed his listening toward Katie. He couldn't find her song. It was like a solid barrier had been erected in her mind. Suddenly, a whirling maelstrom of rage and hate sent him reeling. Majell! His listening had alerted her to his presence. Nathan struggled to push her out of his mind, desperately wishing stubbornness hadn't prevented him from asking Uncle Nevill about shielding.

Icy fingers probed and stabbed his mind, exposing and distorting Nathan's song, leaving him powerless. Torches dimmed to mere spots of yellow light as blackness crept over his eyes. Desolation flooded Nathan's body. How had he ever thought he could help Tegarron? Thought he could defeat Majell. He wanted truth? Truth was that he was good for nothing and nobody. He couldn't even help himself let alone anyone else. Dad knew that. Truth was...there was no truth.

A small pinpoint of white light penetrated Nathan's blindness. Uncaring, he ignored it, but the light persisted. It began to pulse and Nathan heard a single sweet, pure note break through the wall of Majell's lies. Katie! Somehow she had found the strength to reach out from beneath Majell's hold.

Slowly the ice receded from Nathan's mind and limbs as he drew warmth from Katie's song. Strength flowed through his body allowing him to force Majell out.

Sing the song of the sword, Katie urged him. Her presence dimmed, flared briefly as she fought to stay, then faded away.

Sing the song of the sword! He couldn't sing. He could only croak. But he had to try. For Katie and Tegarron, he had to try. He took several deep breaths and directed his listening inward. With a shock, Nathan discovered his song had changed. As it always would, he realized. His song would be constantly rewritten and reshaped, as he himself changed.

Searching, he easily found the memory of the sword's song and opened his mouth. *Croak!* Damn! Why did he think he could sing? Fingernails screeching down a blackboard sounded better than he did. Frantically, Nathan searched for the sword's song again and this time found the songs of Uncle Nevill, Myrrd and Katie wrapped around his own song, their voices lending him strength. Down Nathan slid into his song until he reached the glowing, white light, and the ancient song poured from his mouth strong and true. Joy surged through him. He had found it! He had found his true voice.

He sang the sword's song and the truth of its allegiance to the High King. It began to glow white, burning into Balddrick's flesh until he screamed and dropped his weapon.

Still singing, Nathan slowly walked into the circle of the Nine Stones toward the High King's sword. Majell's warriors shifted uneasily but no order was given to them to move. Suddenly,

Nathan felt the hair on his head stand up and the ground throb beneath his feet. With a wrenching wail, the earth in front of him split open and shivering, hideous wraiths slithered between Nathan and the sword.

A screech from the sky above whipped Nathan's head up to see a black crow wheeling above the Nine Stones, the white patch on its head glistening. Majell!

The sky boiled and churned blood-red. Blue lightning tore through the clouds and slammed into the earth with deafening blasts, hurling Majell's men from their feet. Nathan fought to stay upright. Somehow he had to reach the sword and give it to Tegarron.

"Wyyvern!" The word echoed from stone to stone, growing in intensity until it became a terrified scream pouring from many throats. "Wyyvern!"

Nathan looked up to see Majell's men pointing horrorstruck into the sky. Where the crow had been a long, black shape took its place, leathery wings beating the air in long downward sweeps. Nathan's mouth fell open. It was the creature pictured on the tapestry hanging in the Great Hall. *Wyyvern*! It dived toward Nathan talons extended and sharp toothed mouth shrieking loudly.

Terrified Nathan threw himself to the ground, curling his body into a small, tight ball. He felt the air shudder as the winged creature passed over him.

He risked a quick glance, and saw Majell's troops milling about in confusion. From between the stones a large figure loped though the circle. Brull! Then he saw Katie, the only spot of stillness in a chaotic world.

She appeared translucent as if life had drained from her and left an empty shell. And that, Nathan realized, was exactly what was happening. Majell was using the girl's power to give birth to her horrible nightmare creature, killing Katie in the process.

Nathan thought frantically. Majell was a ShapeChanger, able to take on whatever form she wished. She had become a Wyyvern but despite its outer form, the creature was truly Majell. And a TruthSinger had the ability to reveal truth.

The Wyyvern began a lazy descent in wide, looping circles to where Nathan crouched, confident its prey could not escape. Nathan waited until it neared, then jumped to his feet, facing the oncoming monster. It streaked toward him. Nathan began to sing, his voice soaring above the creature's terrible cries.

White light exploded, illuminating the Nine Stones, then leapt high into the sky fed by Nathan's song. It surrounded the Wyyvern, pulling the winged creature down. Screams of fury battered Nathan, but he continued singing until the Wyyvern plummeted from the clouds and lay twitching at his feet. Wings and claws slowly shriveled and disappeared, leaving behind a bent, old hag huddled in the dirt. The true Majell.

Nathan stumbled into the circle and picked up the sword. He carried it to where Tegarron lay and wrapped the boy's fingers about the hilt. Turning he saw Brull holding a limp Katie in his arms. Was she dead?

The wraiths suddenly swarmed over Majell and Llien and dragged them into the dark hole from which Majell had spawned them. E-V-I-L L-I-V-E. The last thing Nathan saw was Llien's fingers moving frantically in the evil warding sign as the earth closed over him. The Nine Stones spun crazily, then blackness.

Chapter 16

NATHAN OPENED HIS EYES TO FIND HIMSELF LYING ON the couch in Uncle Nevill's study. Home! Then he remembered. He had fainted, swooned, fallen flat on his face. Just once he'd like to be the conquering hero.

"He's awake," Katie said.

Nathan quickly closed his eyes, feigning sleep. He couldn't face her right now.

"He really is awake," she insisted.

Sighing, Nathan opened his eyes. He quickly raised his head, then fell back as pain shot through it. Myrrd unfolded himself from a chair and put a hand behind Nathan's shoulder, helping him sit up. Uncle Nevill beamed and handed him a cup of tea.

"Four sugars," he said.

"What day is it?" Nathan asked. "How long were we gone?"

"About five minutes," Katie told him. "It's the same day we left."

"You're okay," Nathan said, suddenly remembering Katie's limp body in Brull's arms.

"I'm fine," she assured him.

"What happened?" he asked. He accepted the Oreo Uncle Nevill pressed into his hand.

"To make a long story short," Myrrd said, "the king is in his rightful place. Thanks to you."

Nathan remembered then the horror of Majell and Llien being dragged into the hole by the wraiths. He shivered, knowing the image would haunt him for a long, long time.

"That was not your doing," Uncle Nevill told him gently. "You sang her truth. She had become one of those creatures. They were merely reclaiming one of their own."

"But Llien?" Nathan asked.

"He had become one of hers," Myrrd said. "I blame myself for that." His face was drawn and haggard. "Perhaps there is some way..." His voice trailed off.

Nathan turned to Katie. Had she come home to stay? He didn't want to ask her, afraid of the answer.

"You saved me this time." Katie gave Nathan one of her brilliant smiles. Nathan grinned back foolishly.

Uncle Nevill cleared his throat and Nathan started. How long had he been staring at Katie? She'd think he liked her and she'd be impossible to live with...if she lived here.

"But why did you go to the Nine Stones?" he asked. "By the way, I had a heck of a time figuring out what Brull was trying to tell me. Did you really have to use backwords?"

"Llien was hovering around me. I didn't want him to know where I had gone. I overheard one of Majell's men telling Llien to take Tegarron's sword to the Nine Stones at dawn. I didn't know then that he planned to replace the king's sword with an ordinary one and give the magic sword to Majell's son. I just knew something fishy was going on up at the Nine Stones so decided I'd be there at dawn, too. I looked for you, but couldn't find you anywhere."

Nathan grimaced remembering his aimless wandering through the woods.

"So I left a message for you with Brull," Katie continued. "Knowing how you love your backwords I didn't think you'd have any trouble figuring it out. I told Tegarron and he decided to come with me. We got away from his guardian by using..." She suddenly stopped.

"The secret passage." Myrrd finished for her.

She cleared her throat nervously. "Tegarron thought if he could settle things with Majell himself, he would earn his people's respect. Make them see him as a king instead of a kid. I thought I could protect him with my magic." She looked sheepishly at Myrrd. "But I guess I wasn't quite as good as I thought. Majell captured us right away. And, well, the rest you know."

They were all silent for a few minutes, lost in their own thoughts.

"I must return," Myrrd said suddenly. "A whole kingdom to be put to rights." He looked questioningly at Katie.

She shook her head and her face became pinched and sallow. She was back in her real life now. "I have to sort out my own time stream here," she said. "Before I try sorting out others."

Tired words, but Nathan *heard* the hope and strength beneath them.

"Will you thank Brull for me?" she asked. "And say hi to Tegarron."

Myrdd smiled. "Of course. I will return shortly," he said, "to continue with your studies." He raised a hand and disappeared.

Nathan stared at the fine droplets of blue mist settling on Uncle Nevill's carpet, hearing the magic's song. It was becoming second nature, listening.

"Well." Uncle Nevill brushed chocolate cookie crumbs from his lap and stood up. "We have work to do. Your efforts were very good, but you both have much to learn before we turn you lose on the time streams," he said briskly.

He smiled at the astonishment on their faces.

"After all, Myrrd and I can't be around forever. Though it certainly feels like we have been." He caught Nathan's alarmed look and waved an arm.

"Not to worry. You won't be burying us tomorrow. But we have to begin your training now. To be WyndCaller and—TruthSinger?"

He looked at Nathan, eyebrows raised inquiringly.

Nathan hesitated a moment, but knew he'd already made up his mind on the hilltop of the Nine Stones. He was a TruthSinger and always would be. Dad—well he'd just have to take Nathan the way he was and if he couldn't...they'd figure something out. He nodded.

Uncle Nevill briskly clapped his hands together and crossed to the shelf of instruments. "No time like the present," he said.

Now? Nathan looked across at Katie, who grinned and shrugged.

Nathan pushed himself from the couch, then stopped. He had seen something. He quickly crossed to the window and looked out. Snow gusted against the pane, swirling the world with white. Why then did the image of black wings linger in his mind?

Nathan shook his head. His imagination, he guessed. It couldn't possibly be a W-O-R-C.

ABOUT THE AUTHOR

Barbara Haworth-Attard lives in London, Ontario, Canada, with her husband and two school-aged sons. Ms Attard's previous novels for young readers, *Dark of the Moon* and *The Three Wishbells* were also published by Roussan Publishers.

ACKNOWLEDGEMENTS

Thank you once again to Kim, Maggie and Norah for their wonderful suggestions. Thank you to J. Graham Adams for letting me pick his musical brain. Thank you to Jane Frydenlund and Kathryn Rhoades of Roussan Publishers Inc. for their ongoing support. Finally, thank you to Joe.